ECHOING
SILENCE

....

THE 2ND BOOK OF THE
ARKANSAS OIL DAYS SERIES

BRENDA HUTCHESON FICKEY

Echoing Silence

by Brenda Hutcheson Fickey

Trade paperback ISBN: 978-1-943294-00-8
Ebook ISBN: 978-1-943294-01-5

Cover design by Martijn van Tilborgh

Echoing Silence is also available on Amazon Kindle, Barnes & Noble Nook and Apple iBooks.

For more information and to purchase more books by Brenda Fickey, visit *BrendaFickey.com.*

CONTENTS

DEDICATION

For Kyle, Keremy, Elizabeth, Michael, Joshua, Emma, Matthew, and William

To my dad, Charles Hutcheson, and in memory of Aunt Mary Neely

ACKNOWLEDGMENTS

Several years ago, I told my dad I wanted to write a book about Granny, his mother. With *Echoing Silence*, there are now two books that are about this fascinating woman. She is the inspiration behind both Granny Rose and Martha Baker. Thank you, Dad and Aunt Mary, for letting me share her with so many. I'd like to thank all of my family, friends, and fans for encouraging me to write this next segment in the Arkansas Oil Days Series. There are too many to name here, who kept asking about the progress. You wouldn't let me wait too long to write it, or give up when things were tough emotionally and the words wouldn't flow.

Thank you, Olivia, for your editing skills and the vision for some of the scenes that needed fresh eyes. Thank you, Jason, for helping me get the manuscript to Olivia on disk, so we could work on the editing long-distance. Thank you, Traci, for your bubbly excitement when I finished segments and you offered feedback. You are the best spokesperson for my books. Thank you, Brent, for allowing me to set up my base of operation in yours and Traci's home till I get my new office. Thank you Kyle, Keremy, Elizabeth, Michael, Joshua, Emma, Matthew, and William for the love you shower on me. You are the reason I want to create good literature for kids.

Thank you, Dad, Mom, and Joni, for your help with the research. You provided information, companionship, and transportation while I was gathering what I needed to make this story possible. Thank you, Kay, for your love and prayers as I make a new life for myself without Bill. You have encouraged me in ways you are unaware of. Thank you, dear sister.

Thank you, Jacob, Sharon, Chris, Stacia, Kalie, Andrew, Alexandra, Lauren, AJ, Jessie, Rachel, and Deb for your input while this story unfolded, from the false starts to the end. Your comments and encouragement kept me focused.

Thank you, Smackover, for a history that is rich and ripe for storytelling.

Thank you, Centennial Christian Academy colleagues and staff, Cross Roads Baptist Church family and friends, and Mississippi Avenue Baptist Church family and friends, for your love, prayers, encouragement, and excitement for what God is doing in my life.

Thank you, Kudu Publishing, for catching my vision and making this book available to children, adults, libraries, and schools everywhere. While *Whispering Darkness* continues to help me with my own grieving, it is because of *Echoing Silence* that I have learned to experience joy, again, since my Bill's death. Your trust in my art is appreciated. I am grateful to you for believing in my career as an author.

CHAPTER 1

"THAT'S ENOUGH. BREAK IT UP right now, boys."

Hank's right fist stopped in mid-air when he heard the booming voice. Everything moved in slow motion as he lifted his eyes toward the familiar sound of his father's angry words. He saw a man approach with a scowl on his face and flashing eyes. Hank ignored the voice and went back to work on the chubby red-haired boy he straddled on the ground. His left fist tightly gripped a wad of green checkered shirt while he watched the other move to hit the boy again. Surprisingly, there was no contact with the already bloody nose. He felt the fabric and buttons of his own shirt strain against his chest as he was lifted off the boy. He pummeled empty air before being unceremoniously set on the ground away from the fight.

"I said that's enough, Hank."

Everything returned to normal speed except for Hank's breathing and shaking body. He slowly stood. For the first time, he saw the children who had watched the fight in the churchyard. They formed a circle around him and Pinky McLeod under the hundred-year-old sweet gum tree. His heaving chest and lungs burned. In frustration, he watched a big man pull Pinky out of his reach. Hank searched the crowd for his two best friends, Daniel

Wagner and Beth Ann Warden, his fingernails jabbing into his already stinging palms. Not willing to challenge the man who easily handled both angry boys, he wiped at his own bloody nose. Somehow Hank had gotten the best of the fourteen-year-old bully from Snow Hill before he heard the words he was sure had come from his dead father's mouth.

Fresh hot anger radiated from Hank's neck and face when the man held out a hand to help Pinky stand up. He could have sworn it was his daddy, but there was something not quite right about the man's build. Hank's heart ached with prickly pangs when he realized Deputy Collins was the man who had spoken and broke up the fight. Pete Collins restrained both struggling boys by their upper arms on either side of his muscular form. Hank's eyes stung with unshed tears. The scent from the deputy's Sunday suit added to the pain of the mistaken identity.

"All right, everybody, it's over. Find your parents," the deputy said.

Hank watched the crowd disperse. Then he saw his mother's face. Her dark blue eyes showed fear and pain. His pounding heart accused him with every aching beat. He had seen that same look in her eyes seven years ago. Back then, it was the letter she had received from the Army that said his daddy was missing after a major battle in France. This time, *he* was the cause. The fight with Pinky suddenly went out of him, replaced with the sharp claws of sorrow and grief stabbing at his guilt-ridden heart.

"Martha, let's go inside the church with this."

Deputy Collins' grip on Hank's upper arm tightened as they marched across the churchyard to the one-room building. They climbed the six steps and entered through the open doors as the congregation filed out. Pastor Bob shook hands with the last two people.

"Can I help, Pete?" he said from the doorway.

"Thanks, Bob, but I think Martha and I can handle it this time. We'll close up for you if you need to go."

"Okay, if you're sure. Let me know if I can do anything. Oh, yeah, will you close the windows? Just in case it rains before next Sunday. Check the one behind the curtain, too. Sometimes I forget that one and critters get in. Take care, now."

Hank heard the deputy chuckle and thought his anger might be fading. At least, he hoped it was.

"We will. Thanks. See you next week."

The noonday heat from the July sun was thick inside the large room, even with all the windows opened. The farther from the door they got, the heavier the air in the church felt. It was hard to catch a good, deep breath. Sweat beaded Hank's hairline and slowly trickled down his back. His shirt stuck to his skin when the deputy forced him and Pinky to sit on the front pew. There were only a couple of feet between them.

Hank thought about his daddy's funeral service just a few weeks ago. It had been hot that day, too. He had worn a black suit then. Today, he wore the new white shirt Ma had made him. It was dirty now, and stained with blood. He took the handkerchief Deputy Collins offered and held it under his nose. His inspection of the tears in the shirt made him wince. He didn't think Ma could fix them easily, if at all. Hank stared at the picture of the Jordan River behind the pulpit, avoiding his ma's eyes and the deputy's face. They sat in chairs across from the boys. *What's wrong with me, Daddy?*

"What was that all about, Hank?" the deputy said.

The silence was deafening.

"Pinky?"

"He attacked me for no reason," Pinky said.

"Is that right, Hank?" Ma said.

He looked at his ma, fresh anger heating his temper.

"I…he…I," Hank said.

"Hank, this is the third fight you've gotten into since the fourth of July picnic two weeks ago. This must stop, son."

"Where are your parents, Pinky?" Deputy Collins said.

"I came alone."

"I don't recall seeing you in church, so why are you here now?"

"Look, I've got a right to defend myself. He doesn't have the right to just up and hit me for no reason. And for your information, I've got a right to be where I want to be."

Hank looked at Pinky with a smirk and snickered. Pinky stood and threw up his fists in a boxing stance. Hank stood, accepting the challenge; but the deputy stepped between them.

"No more," Deputy Collins said. "Hank, I want you to shake hands with Pinky."

Hank looked at the deputy with hot, defiant eyes.

"No."

"Henry Stuart Baker, you do what you're told," Ma said.

"I *won't* and *he* can't make me, Ma."

Hank turned to leave, but Deputy Collins blocked his path.

"Sit down, Hank." The strained control in the deputy's behavior made Hank pause a moment. *He reminds me of Daddy so much.*

"You aren't my father."

Hank heard his ma's gasp and looked at her. The hurt, worried look shot flaming arrows at him; but he didn't care this time.

"I may not be your father, but you will *not* speak to your mother like that again in my presence, young man. Now, sit down."

Hank's chest heaved in the heat from his labored breathing. Sweat stung his eyes. He forced his tightly clenched fists to stay at his sides and the nerves in his knees and legs trembled. He stared at Deputy Collins without flinching. *Who do you think you are?* No one moved or said anything for a long, slow minute of thunderous silence. Hank returned to his seat, intently watching the deputy's hard face.

"Let's go, Pinky. I'm taking you home. Go home with your ma and brother, Hank. We'll all have a talk when I get there."

Without another word, the meeting was over. Hank ran down the aisle and out the door like a prisoner on the run.

"Hank," Ma said. "Where are you going?"

He jumped all six steps in a single bound and blindly ran through the cemetery gate. The markers blurred as he raced through the rows of graves, till he reached his daddy's. The dirt was dried and cracked from the heat. Hank fell to his knees and punched the hardened soil with agonized sorrow.

"Why did you have to die? Where are you when I need you?"

He heard running and turned, silently waiting for Daniel and Beth Ann to join him. Daniel's smile was all teeth, but Beth Ann had worry lines between her brows.

"What a fight!" Daniel said.

Beth Ann punched him on the upper arm.

"Hey, what did you do that for?" He rubbed the muscle and rotated his shoulder. They knelt on either side of Hank.

"Can't you see he's hurting?" Beth Ann said. "Hank, are you okay?"

"You sure got the best of Pinky McLeod. What was that all about anyway?"

Daniel flinched when Beth Ann drew back her fist again.

"Can you both come to my place later this afternoon?" Hank said.

"Are you in a lot of trouble?" Daniel said.

"Meet me in the loft, and I'll explain everything," Hank said. "But you can't tell anyone."

"I'll be there. How about you, Daniel?"

"Sure. I'll come over as soon as I finish eating. My folks won't make a fuss about being gone if I eat first."

"Good," Hank said. "Go straight to the loft. I'll meet you there as soon as I can. I really need your help."

"You know you can count on us," Beth Ann said, putting a hand on his shoulder.

Daniel put a hand on his other shoulder.

"Yeah, we make a pretty good team."

CHAPTER 2

Hank watched Deputy Collins open the truck door for his ma. He was a little light headed and his legs trembled when he stood with his friends. Jimmy Jack was already in the back of the truck. He saw the deputy kiss his ma on the cheek before he and Pinky walked to his Model T sedan. He motioned for Pinky to sit in the back seat.

"Come on, Hank. It's time to go," Ma said. She was angry now, the hurt gone from her voice.

"She sounds really mad, Hank," Daniel said.

"Yeah. See you guys later."

The three friends silently walked out of the cemetery together, going their separate ways just outside the gate. Hank climbed into the cab of the truck. Dread replaced his own anger.

"I hope you didn't plan to go fishing with Daniel this afternoon. Your behavior is not giving me confidence in your best judgment right now. We've got a lot to discuss, young man."

"Ma, he had no right to talk to me that way."

"Who didn't? Pinky or Pete? I don't understand what's gotten into you lately. What's happened between you and Pete since the funeral?"

Hank didn't say anything. He just looked out the side window. His thoughts were not on the impending confrontation with Ma and Deputy Collins, but on the meeting with Daniel and Beth Ann later. Even with the preoccupation, he couldn't ignore all his ma had said. The short ride home was the longest of Hank's life.

He had sworn to honor his daddy's memory at the gravesite ceremony and to be the man he would want him to be in his place. *That includes defending my friends and family, doesn't it? I have a responsibility to protect us, don't I? That's what you would do, Daddy. It's what you did when you went off to war, wasn't it?*

Corporal Charles Henry Baker had died in the last major battle of World War I, the Battle of Belleau Wood. He had died defending a family near the front lines. His body was discovered nearly seven years later when the family returned to their farm and began the restoration of the barn. Corporal Baker had been declared missing in action until then. He was given full military honors at his funeral and received the Silver Star for bravery posthumously. Hank kept the medal in a special frame on the table by his bed. The flag Ma was given at the funeral was framed along with a picture of Daddy in full dress uniform. It hung on the wall above the fireplace in the front sitting room.

Ma and Deputy Collins had become friends before she knew what had happened to Daddy. Since the funeral, it was getting to be more than just a friendship in Hank's mind. As the weeks passed, Deputy Collins seemed to come to the house more often. He made repairs around the farm and helped with the crops when he wasn't on duty. He took more meals with them and drove them to Camden from time to time to get supplies that weren't available in Smackover.

Is Deputy Collins taking your place, Daddy?

Jimmy Jack took to Deputy Collins as if he were their daddy.

"I like him, Hank. Why don't you?" Jimmy Jack had said. "I don't have a daddy like you do. *You* remember him. *I* can't. So it's like *you* have a daddy, but *I* don't. I want a daddy like you have. When I look at Deputy Collins, I see Daddy."

Hank resisted Deputy Collins' friendship until after the funeral. He watched him help Ma get through that whole time. Eventually, Hank grew to appreciate the deputy's relationship with their family.

At the gravesite, you promised Daddy you'd show Deputy Collins the respect that was due an adult, a community protector, and a friend. So what's happened?

Hank was startled that his own words haunted him just now. It wasn't Daddy's voice taunting him and reminding him of promises not kept. Hank suddenly realized he hadn't heard his daddy's voice since they had buried him. Angry tears flooded his eyes and rolled down his cheeks.

Stop crying, Hank. You're twelve years old, for crying out loud. Be the man your daddy was and would want you to be.

Hank sniffed and wiped his nose on the top of his sleeve.

What do I know about being a man? What do I know about you, Daddy? What would you do in my situation? I don't know anymore. I don't know you like I thought I did. How am I supposed to know how to be like you when I don't know who you really are? You're gone. I won't ever know you like I want to. In fact, I'm really no different from Jimmy Jack where you are concerned, now that I think about it.

"Are you coming in?" Ma said.

They were home. How long had they just sat in the truck before she said anything? He opened the door and slowly got out, walking toward the barn.

"Where are you going?"

"I'll be in the loft."

"Make sure you hear me when I call you to dinner. It will only take about half an hour."

He walked faster toward the barn, willing himself not to run.

"Hank, wait," Jimmy Jack said. "I'll come with you."

"Just leave me alone, Jimmy Jack."

He ran to the barn and quickly climbed the ladder. The barn door creaked within seconds of his reaching the loft.

"Hank?"

"Go away."

His brother's soft steps on the ladder annoyed him. The smell of hot hay stung his nostrils till he opened both windows in the loft. A cross-breeze caused him to shudder as his sweaty shirt cooled. He looked out over the back acreage of the Baker property, wishing he were alone to think.

"Are you all right?"

"Why wouldn't I be?" Hank sniffed and hurriedly wiped his nose on his shirtsleeve. "What do you want, anyway?"

"What were you and Pinky fighting about?"

"I can't tell you right now, maybe never."

"Why not?" Jimmy Jack joined Hank at the window.

"It's not safe."

"But if you're in danger, you need to tell Mr. Pete. He can help you."

"I don't want his help, and you'd better not say anything to him, either."

"But..."

"Leave it be, Jimmy Jack. I'll take care of it myself."

"Everyone knows he's a bully, Hank. I don't want you to get hurt. I don't want to see Ma be sad because you got hurt. She's been sad long enough."

"I know. I'll be all right. Pinky won't hurt me if he knows what's good for him."

"Why won't you let Mr. Pete help?"

"It's not his responsibility. I've got to do it myself. It's what Daddy would want."

Jimmy Jack gently laid a hand on his big brother's shoulder.

"Daddy would want you to fight Pinky McLeod?"

"He would if he knew what it was about."

"Hank, you're scaring me."

"Don't worry, little brother. I've got a plan."

"Can I help?"

"I'll let you know. For now, just stay close to Ma. And remember, don't tell Deputy Collins."

"Okay, Hank. I'll take care of her; and I won't say anything to anybody, not even Mr. Pete. I won't let you down."

They heard a motor car pull up under the sweet gum tree near the front of the house. Both boys ran to the other window and saw the deputy's big black sedan.

"Let's get to the house," Hank said. "Ma will be calling us to dinner any minute now."

****

It was the quietest Sunday dinner Hank had remembered eating in a while. The tension in the air was as thick as Ma's freshly churned butter. The fried chicken was a golden brown, just like Hank liked it; but he couldn't taste any of his food. The anticipation of the family meeting after dinner left a bitter taste in his mouth that wouldn't go away.

"Hank, are you going to eat or just push your food around on your plate?" Ma said.

He shoved a large bite of mashed potatoes and gravy into his mouth. It may as well have been a boll of cotton. There was no flavor to it at all.

"Jimmy Jack, aren't you hungry, son?" Pete said.

"Just thinking."

"About what?" the deputy said. He tried to sound lighthearted, but his voice still had an edge to it.

"I was just wondering why Pinky McLeod likes bullying people around."

Hank swallowed hard and gave Jimmy Jack a burning glare.

"It doesn't matter whether he's a bully or not," Ma said. "We shouldn't behave like he does, no matter what."

"Why the interest in Pinky?" Pete said.

Hank kicked at Jimmy Jack under the table, barely fanning his brother's dangling feet.

"Just wondering, I guess. Ma, is Hank a bully, too?"

"What on earth would make you ask that?" Ma said.

"Well…"

"I'm not a bully, Jimmy Jack. I was fighting Pinky for protection. There's a difference," Hank said. Heat instantly radiated from every nerve in his body. He squirmed in his seat at the startling slip of his tongue.

"For protection?" Ma said. "Hank, what are you talking about?"

He shrank back into his chair when everyone stopped eating and stared at him. Pete set his fork down, scooting his chair back.

"Martha, you and Jimmy Jack finish your meals. Give us a few minutes, will you? Hank, let's go to the sitting room."

"Eat your dinner before it gets cold, son," Ma said. "There's peach cobbler for dessert."

"Yes, ma'am."

Hank was relieved his brother was so excited about cobbler, but Ma's shaky voice troubled him. Deputy Collins followed him to the sitting room, where they sat on each end of the sofa. Neither spoke immediately. The deputy propped his elbows on his knees, resting his chin on the tops of his clasped hands. The ticking of the grandfather clock grew loud until Pete broke the silence, his tone calmer than Hank expected.

"Did Pinky threaten you today? Is that why you were fighting?"

Silence.

"You just said you were fighting Pinky for protection. As an officer of the law and, more importantly, as your friend, I'd like to know what kind of protection you think you needed to give that brought about a brawl in the churchyard."

Silence.

"If something happens to you or your family, how do you think I would feel, especially if I could have prevented it if you had told me?"

"It's not your responsibility."

"Why not?"

"It's not about you, Deputy Collins."

"Then who's it about, Hank?

"Me."

"You? I don't understand."

"I didn't attack Pinky. He attacked me."

"Why? Why would Pinky attack you?"

"Because…"

Heavy footfalls tramped across the front porch before someone pounded on the front door. Through the screen, Hank saw Abraham, his round eyes were a stark white against his dark skin.

"Hank! Deputy Collins! Someone! Help!"

CHAPTER 3

PETE RUSHED TO THE DOOR to let Abraham in. A foreboding filled Hank's heart, not unlike when he saw the government sedan in their driveway last month. Hank stood by his friend.

"Abraham, what's wrong?" Pete said.

"Sir, it's Granny Rose. She's…she's…"

"Whoa, now. Slow down, boy. What about Granny Rose?"

"I think she's dead!"

"What?" Hank said.

Ma quickly joined them in the sitting room.

"What's going on in here?" she said.

"Ma, it's Granny Rose," Hank said.

"Pete? What are you standing here for? Go!"

"Hank, stay with your mother, son. We'll finish our discussion when I get back. Martha, I'll be back as soon as I can."

Abraham and the deputy left in a cloud of dust as the sedan sped toward the road.

"Hank, you're as white as a ghost. What happened?"

"Abraham said Granny Rose is dead."

Tears streamed down Hank's face. Ma wrapped him in a warm embrace.

"Shh…Hank, you're trembling all over. It's going to be okay. Honey, let's not jump to conclusions till we know all the facts."

****

Daniel and Beth Ann were out of breath when they climbed the ladder to the hayloft nearly an hour later. Hank was already there. He didn't take his attention off the tree line in the direction of Granny Rose's farm.

"We ran all the way from the road," Beth Ann said. "I don't think we were seen. Boy, am I glad to see you're already here." Both of Hank's friends stood on either side of him at the window.

"What are we looking at?" Daniel said.

"Abraham came over earlier to get Deputy Collins. He said Granny Rose was dead."

"What?" Beth Ann said. "That must be what the big emergency with my dad was all about just before I left to come here. Deputy Collins had come over in a tizzy, and they left together in a big hurry. I thought it was about you, Hank. I didn't think about Granny Rose. Don't worry, though, I don't think she's dead. My dad wouldn't have been in such a hurry if she were dead. At least, he isn't in a hurry when he goes to see about anyone who really is dead."

"Funny, I never put death and Granny Rose together before. I just assumed she couldn't die," Daniel said.

"How do you figure that?" Beth Ann said.

"Well, she's been around forever, hasn't she? Does anyone know how old she really is? How do we know she was ever born? After all, she *can* cast spells on people and all."

"Daniel, that's crazy," Beth Ann said. "What is your obsession with Granny Rose? Of course, she was born *and* she can die. She's as human as the three of us are."

"How would you know? Were you there when she was born?"

"Would you listen to yourself? She's a nice lady who…"

"It's my fault," Hank said.

"Your fault?" Daniel said. "That's not good. Do you know what kind of trouble you'll be in, if she *is* alive and she finds out *you* were responsible for what happened to her?"

Beth Ann reached around Hank and punched Daniel in the upper arm.

"Ow! What was that for?"

"How is Granny Rose's situation your fault, Hank?" Beth Ann said.

He turned and sat in the hay under the window. They joined him.

"I guess we'd best get down to business. I asked you to come here because I need your help. I can't go to Sheriff Stan or get Deputy Collins involved without putting them and my family in danger."

"Does this have to do with Pinky and the fight today?" Beth Ann said.

Hank nodded slowly, staring straight ahead.

"He said I'd better…"

What am I doing? How do I know I'm not putting them in danger, too?

"He said you'd better what, Hank?" Beth Ann said.

They heard a motor car pull up in the drive. In unison, the three friends ran to the window in time to see Deputy Collins get out of his sedan.

"Stay here while I find out what happened," Hank said.

"We'll be waiting," Beth Ann said.

Hank ran to the house, his heart pounding. When he entered the kitchen from the back door, he heard voices in the front room. He stopped briefly to catch his breath. Ma, Jimmy Jack, and the deputy were walking down the hallway toward him.

"Will she be all right?" Ma said.

"I think so. She just needs to rest and not do so much," Pete said. "Abraham is such a blessing around the place, but it's just too big for the two of them to work alone."

"What are you going to do?"

"I don't know, yet. One thing's for sure, I can't let her work that place alone. And one hand isn't enough to help out, either. She's one stubborn Indian. She won't like me interfering, but it's too dangerous for her."

Hank watched them with anxious anticipation.

"What happened? Did I hear you right? Granny Rose is alive?" Hank said.

They all took seats around the table. The grandfather clock in the sitting room chimed the four o'clock hour.

"Yes, Hank, she's alive. Abraham said they were picking plums when they heard a gunshot close by, probably bootleggers. At the same time, Granny collapsed from what Doc Warden is pretty sure was a mild heart attack. Abraham assumed she had been shot. He was afraid to check, for fear someone would think *he* had shot her. He was afraid he'd go to jail without being allowed to explain what really happened. So he came over here for help instead."

"Oh, Pete," Ma said. "He must have been scared to death. It's getting to where a body can't be safe in your own yard with these stills and bootleggers all about. Will you and Stan be looking into the shooting later today or tomorrow?"

"It'll wait till early tomorrow. Stan said we'd go out between midnight and daybreak to check it out. He doesn't think they'll move the still while it's brewing. We can't think of any other reason for the shooting. I'm just glad Abraham trusted us enough to not run off. Hank, I have you to thank for that. You're a real friend to him, son. You both made a real difference today."

Hank nodded and watched Ma take the deputy's hand in both of hers.

"I almost lost my grandmother today, Martha." The deputy cleared his throat. "She's the only family I have left."

Hank watched Ma embrace the deputy while he cried. Hank silently admired his love for Granny. He understood the deputy's compassion. That thought startled him for a moment. *This is not the time to think about that right now. We've got to stop Pinky.* He quietly left through the back door without disturbing Ma and the deputy. His resolve grew stronger with every step. Hank was determined to stop Pinky McLeod, but he needed the help of his best friends to pull it off. Halfway to the barn, the screen door to the back porch slammed.

"Hank, where are you going?" Jimmy Jack said.

He stopped and turned toward his little brother.

"I'm going to the barn to finish some chores, Jimmy Jack. Go on back to the house. It won't take me much longer."

Hank turned and ran the rest of the way to the barn. Daniel and Beth Ann were waiting where he'd left them. He hurriedly latched the door.

"We've got to stop Pinky," Hank said. He climbed the ladder two rungs at a time.

They all sat in a tight circle in the middle of the loft.

"You're the only ones I trust to help me. Lives will depend on us, so you can't tell anyone about our plan."

"Whoa!" Daniel said. "This is way bigger than I thought."

"We won't tell, will we?" Beth Ann said.

"Uh-uh. Tell us why you were fighting Pinky today."

"Just listen," Hank said. "You'll understand when I finish."

"Okay," Daniel said.

"Have either of you noticed the sky at night lately?"

Daniel and Beth Ann looked at one another. Daniel shrugged and shook his head.

"What's the sky got to do with Pinky?" Beth Ann said.

"You haven't noticed a bright glow in the sky late at night?"

"You're the only person I know of who doesn't sleep all night. When do you see the sky glow?" Daniel said.

"It's usually really late. I've noticed it's out toward Beech Hill mostly. It lights up the sky above the trees like a dancing, glowing, yellow light. I guess if you don't know what to look for you could miss it."

"Isn't that where Abraham's family moved to?" Beth Ann said.

"Oh, yeah, I forgot about that," Daniel said.

"Pinky told me I broke the law when I helped Abraham stay here. He said that Abraham needed to be set straight. When I told him I hadn't broken any laws and that Abraham was my friend, he called me a traitor. He said I would have to be set straight, too. Telling Sheriff Stan is useless because he said the law was on his side. Then he said Granny Rose, and anyone standing with her, would get what's coming to them if she didn't stop protecting Abraham. Pinky said that her being friends with the wrong kinds of people makes her no better than they are. He said he and his night friends would show her the light if they had to."

"What's that supposed to mean, 'night friends'?" Beth Ann said. "And who doesn't belong here?"

"According to Pinky, anyone who comes here to take jobs away from the locals and who meddle in places they don't have a right to be. Daniel, do you remember what you told me about how lots of people don't consider the deaths of colored people important enough to investigate?"

"Yeah, is that how Pinky and his night friends think?"

"That's my impression," Hank said. "I think the light he's talking about is the glow in the sky. Anyone getting in the way of their mission to rid the area of undesirables gets a visit to show them the light."

"But, what can we do?" Beth Ann said. "Granny Rose doesn't take well to people telling her what to do and what not to do. Not without her shotgun, anyway."

"She can take care of herself pretty well, if you ask me," Daniel said.

"Not anymore. Deputy Collins said Doc told him she had a heart attack today. She's got to rest, not do so much anymore. It's too much for Abraham, too."

"But we're just kids," Beth Ann said. "We can't stop Pinky and his friends by ourselves."

"Look, if Clyde Byrd, practically a kid himself, can be the mayor of Smackover and clean that place up, why can't we take care of Granny Rose and Abraham?" Hank said.

"Isn't he called the 'boy mayor' or something like that?" Daniel said.

"Yeah, my dad knows his dad. He's a doctor, too."

"Well, if he can be tough on crime in Smackover, why can't we stand tough against Pinky and his night friends? Daniel, Beth Ann, we have work to do. I need your help to protect Abraham and Granny Rose. Are you with me?"

Beth Ann smiled at Daniel and nodded.

"We're in," Daniel said. "Sherlock Holmes and Dr. Watson are on the case with you." Suddenly his smile faded. His eyebrows shot up, and his eyes looked as if they would pop out of his head. "Hey, wait a minute. Just how do you suggest we protect Granny Rose? Are we going to have to stay with her all day *and* all night?"

"Hank, I want to help, too," Jimmy Jack said.

"Ahhh!" Daniel said.

CHAPTER 4

ALL THREE STOOD IN UNISON and stared with wide eyes toward the top of the ladder. Hank's voice was stuck in his throat. Their conversation had been so intense, and Jimmy Jack had been so quiet that none of them heard him unlatch the barn door. Hank swallowed hard before he could speak.

"What did you hear, Jimmy Jack," Hank said.

Jimmy Jack stepped into the loft.

"I heard it all, Hank. I want to help take care of Granny Rose and Abraham, too."

Daniel sat with his knees drawn up to his chest, his arms crossed over his knees, and his forehead on his arms for a moment.

"You scared half my life away, Jimmy Jack" he said.

"We may as well include him, Hank," Beth Ann said. "What's your plan?"

"Well, it's gone now. Whatever plan had *been* in my brain just got scared clean away, thanks to *you*, Jimmy Jack. If you're going to help, you have to do exactly what we say and don't tell anyone, you hear?"

"Okay."

"Promise you won't tell? Cross your heart and hope to die?"

Jimmy Jack's eyebrows shot up over large, round eyes. He took a deep breath, not answering too quickly; then he nodded.

"I promise."

"Cross your heart and spit in your hand promise?" Hank said.

Jimmy Jack crossed his heart.

"I promise."

He spit in his palm and shook Hank's hand.

"Wow, that's a serious oath," Daniel said.

"All right, everybody," Hank said. "Let's meet at Catfish Haven tomorrow afternoon. Plan to stay a while. I have a feeling I'm going to have enough chores to keep me busy till lunchtime, if not longer, when Ma and Deputy Collins get finished with me tonight. I'll have a plan by then."

"Okay, see you guys there," Beth Ann said.

"Till tomorrow," Daniel said.

"We don't need anyone else snooping around while we're all up here. Let's go, Jimmy Jack, before Ma or Deputy Collins comes looking for us."

****

The family meeting took place around the table after supper dishes were put away. Hank was glad Jimmy Jack was already in bed.

"Hank, we've got some unfinished business about your behavior earlier today in the churchyard," Deputy Collins said.

"Son, we're not ganging up on you; but I'm very disappointed in you right now," Ma said. "Why are you fighting all of a sudden?"

"You wouldn't understand, Ma," Hank said.

"Understand or not, you need to tell me what's going on that you think you have to fight your way through whatever is bothering you?" Ma said.

Silence.

"Are you going to answer her, Hank? Earlier today, you said something about Pinky attacking you. What was that all about?"

"Pinky attacked you?"

"He…" Hank slid his sweaty hands along his trousers leg and drew in a shaky breath.

"He what?" Ma said.

Hank looked from the deputy to his ma. His lower lip trembled and tears swelled to overflowing from both his eyes, down his cheeks. He wiped them angrily with the back of his hands.

"You *wouldn't understand*, Ma." Hank's heart wrenched a hot pain. He didn't mean to sound harsh.

"I will *not* have you taking your anger out on your ma, Hank. You *will* talk with a respectful tone. What would your father say or do if he heard you speak to her that way?"

Hank's chest heaved with each breath. His angry eyes burned as he looked from his ma to the deputy and back. He spoke through clenched jaws to keep his teeth from clattering as if he were cold.

"I'm sorry, Ma. I…I…"

Hank covered his eyes with his hands, hiding from his ma's face. His elbows on the table kept his shaking arms steady.

"I can't explain why I'm behaving like I am. I'm trying not to, but…"

Pete's warm hand kneaded Hank's shoulder.

"You need to tell me why Pinky attacked you," the deputy said. "And if he did, how is it you ended up looking like the one on the attack?"

Hank looked sharply from Ma to Deputy Collins and shoved the hand off his shoulder.

"You don't believe me."

"I didn't say that."

"You don't have to. I can see it in your face."

"Hank, this is just the behavior I was talking about," Ma said. "What is wrong, son?"

"I don't know, Ma. Nothing. Everything. I just don't know. It's like I have no control over myself anymore." Hank's words felt like punches in his stomach. "Pinky kept saying stuff about Daddy. Then when I wouldn't light into him, he said stuff about you and Deputy Collins. I tried to walk away, but he wouldn't leave me be. Daddy always said not to start a fight; but he also told me not to let anyone just beat me up, either. He threw the first punch. I guess I just snapped because all I kept hearing was the stuff he said, over and over inside my head."

"Hank…"

"I *knew* you wouldn't understand. Just tell me what my punishment is and let me go to bed, *please*."

"All right, son. Go on to bed. Pete and I will talk about your punishment and let you know in the morning."

Hank noisily pushed his chair back, nearly knocking it over, and bolted for his room. It took every ounce of self-control to shut his bedroom door quietly. He didn't want to wake his brother. He crept to the open window and sat on the sill, watching the fireflies playing in the shadows of the woods at the edge of the Baker property. He turned his attention to the road that led to the church.

If he won't come to me, I'll go to him.

Hank slipped out the window to the soft grass below, allowing his eyes to adjust to the darkness before creeping from the house to the open field. He took the shortcut to the cemetery. The sky was clear, and the bright moon allowed him to see without a lantern. He noticed the many layers of stars away from the moon's glow, and could see the farthest ones faintly twinkling in the distant heavens.

Hank found the cemetery easily and jumped the fence near the back row. No matter how hot the weather, he realized it was always cold where the dead lay in the ground. He shivered as he searched the markers for the gap where his father's fresh grave was. He carefully walked around the final resting-places of several local people. He finally found the one that belonged to Corporal Charles Baker, Hank's idol and the town's fallen hero. He sat on the ground where his father's head lay, and searched the darkness that matched his soul.

How far away is heaven? He tried to recall if the preacher had ever said anything in a sermon to answer that question. He pulled grass out of the ground at his sides and tossed the blades away.

"Is that why I can't hear you anymore, Daddy? Is it so far away you can't hear or even see me? How could you put yourself in so much danger that you wouldn't come home to us? Why did that family's farm mean more to you than we did? Than I did? How am I supposed to take care of Ma and Jimmy Jack without you?"

Hank lay prostrate beside the dirt mound and sobbed uncontrollably till the grief passed several minutes later. Not able to cry anymore, he sat with his legs crossed, his back bowed. He threw some dirt clumps toward the sound of a cricket a couple of graves to his right.

"How am I supposed to protect us from the likes of Pinky McLeod? If he's not saying things that are really awful about Ma and you or Ma and Deputy Collins, he's threatening me and my friends. What am I supposed to do?" He waited, hoping for a response. Instead, he kept picturing the deputy in his mind.

"What really hurts is how much like you Deputy Collins is. It's down right scary. But he's not you. I listen, but I can't hear you anymore. Did you know that? I hear his voice and think it's yours. If it weren't for the pictures of you, I don't think I'd remember what you looked like. Do you know how angry that makes me? I look around at other kids and watch them with both of their parents. Then I look at our family and see a hole. You're supposed to be here with us, not in the ground. I'm so jealous of those other kids, even Daniel and Beth Ann. I *hate* how I feel. I *hate* that I don't have a daddy. I *hate* that Ma is alone. I *hate* that I hate. You used to always say that hatred is a terrible way to feel, but I *hate* right now." Hank drew a ragged breath.

"I don't know how I feel about you right now. I love you so much, but…I feel so lost without you. Jimmy Jack doesn't know you. Ma used to be lonely, but I don't think she is anymore. I don't know how I feel about Deputy Collins either. Ma likes him a lot. Jimmy Jack likes him, too. I could use a daddy right now, but you're not here. Who's going to teach me what you didn't? Who's going to help me become a man? Who's going to teach me about life? That was your job. *Why* did God have to take you away from me? What did I do to make him do that? What do I have to do to get him to bring you back to me? You know what? I *hate* God. And I *hate* you for letting him do this to me."

The noise of horses galloping through the woods behind the cemetery startled Hank. He crouched low and hid behind a marker near Corporal Baker's grave. Flashes of floating lights cast a yellow tinge on several white, ghost-like apparitions.

"Those aren't fireflies."

He pressed himself flat against the stone, listening for voices. He looked at the sky above the trees in the direction the horses came from. A yellow, dancing glow faintly lit the sky. He froze when he heard his name whispered from the other side of his father's grave.

"Are you all right, son?"

"Daddy?"

CHAPTER 5

"HANK, ARE YOU ALL RIGHT?" the deputy said. The whisper was barely audible.

"Yeah. What are you doing here?"

"I thought you'd be here, so I came to take you home. Your ma is really worried."

"I know. I didn't mean to scare her. I just needed to talk to you, uh, him."

Hank heard the deputy move closer.

"Did you hear and see that in the woods just now?" Hank said.

"Yeah, I need to get you home so I can check it out."

"I'll be all right. Go on. I'll get home okay."

"Are you crazy? Your ma would have my hide if she knew I had found you and let you do that, especially with all that's happened."

"I won't tell if you won't."

"That's not the way it works, Hank. Not when you love someone. You don't keep secrets from those you love."

"But…"

"No. I'm taking you home, first."

****

Hank got up when the rooster crowed. The sun was just coming up. He had a lot of chores to do, besides the ones on the list Ma and Deputy Collins made up before they discovered him missing. Deputy Collins told Ma where Hank had been. She took pity on him and decided not to add to his punishment. Hank was very thankful, especially after seeing the list. It was long enough that he thought he might not be finished in time to meet Daniel and Beth Ann at the fishing hole later that afternoon. Just as she had done when Hank spent a couple of weeks working for Granny Rose last month, Ma had set out his breakfast before going to bed herself. He ate both bacon and egg biscuits then got started.

Hank had plenty of opportunity to plan a strategy for protecting Abraham and Granny Rose *and* facing Pinky, if it went that far. Convincing Daniel to go along with some of the plan would be harder than Beth Ann. He was confident that Daniel would see the benefits and come around. The trick was finding something for Jimmy Jack to do. He needed to stay at home and out of harm's way. The biggest problem would be convincing Ma and Deputy Collins to go along with it without making them suspicious.

Before any action could be taken, they needed to collect enough information to know if Pinky was a real threat. Daniel and Beth Ann had been really good at getting information in the past. He knew they would be successful again. This time, Hank planned to be more directly involved. Since there wasn't a skeleton hiding in the loft, he was free to come and go without the fear of Ma discovering anything she shouldn't. Once they knew exactly what to expect, they could put the plan into action.

Dividing the different parts of the investigation was the first order of business. Jimmy Jack's job would be to make sure he knew where Ma was at all times. When Deputy Collins was around, he would make sure the deputy didn't interfere with the others. He could ask the deputy to go fishing at their secret fishing hole, if he wanted. It was a sacrifice Hank was willing to make.

Beth Ann needed to use her interest in medicine to find out what kinds of emergencies her father had treated in the last few weeks. Then she would be her father's assistant at Granny Rose's when they were there.

Daniel would be in charge of finding out who was part of any nighttime activity in the woods. He would need to learn as much about any Beech Hill activity that could explain the glow in the sky.

Hank would go to Snow Hill and learn what he could about Pinky's night friends and their activities. The plan was to gather information and report back to the loft by the end of the week. Helping Abraham and Granny Rose would be easier once they knew exactly what they were up against.

****

It was late afternoon when Hank and Jimmy Jack approached the rock above the secret fishing hole they called Catfish Haven. They could hear Daniel and Beth Ann long before they came around the rock.

"You know, Daniel, you scream just like a girl," Beth Ann said.

"No, I don't."

"Yes, you do. When Jimmy Jack scared us yesterday, you sounded just like my mom when she sees a mouse."

"I didn't mean to scare you," Jimmy Jack said.

Hank heard Daniel suck in air and watched him jerk his fishing pole, nearly hitting himself between the eyes. He giggled quietly. It felt good to laugh. It had been quite a while since he had laughed out loud.

"Don't scream, Daniel, it's just Jimmy Jack and me," Hank said. "I thought you would have heard us. We made enough noise to wake the dead."

"Yeah, well…"

"Don't worry, Jimmy Jack," Beth Ann said. "Daniel's always jumpy. Come on up. We just got here ourselves. Let's do some fishing."

"Wow, you're the only girl I know who likes fishing and putting worms on your own hook and stuff."

"I'll take that as a compliment, Jimmy Jack."

"Call me, Jimmy. I really don't like being called Jimmy Jack. I always feel like I'm in trouble. When Hank's in trouble, Ma calls him Henry Stuart. He's really in trouble when she does that. I'm tired of people calling me Jimmy Jack all the time."

"What's wrong with Jimmy Jack?" Hank said. "It's a perfectly good name. Did you know Daddy gave you that name? It was his brother's name."

"I didn't know you had an Uncle Jimmy Jack," Daniel said.

"We don't. He died of a fever before he was a year old. Daddy really liked being a big brother, but he never got to be one. So he named you 'Jimmy Jack,' Jimmy Jack."

"All the same, I want people to start calling me Jimmy, just Jimmy.

"That's kind of creepy, being named for a dead kid," Daniel said.

"Don't give him any ideas, Daniel. He needs to sleep alone at night."

"I thought you wanted to be called George, Beth Ann," Jimmy Jack said. "I haven't heard anybody call you that in a while."

"Well, I guess I've outgrown it. I got tired of people rolling their eyes at me all the time. I'm going to be a doctor whether I have a boy's name or my own. Why change who I am?"

"I guess that makes sense," Jimmy Jack said.

"Woo-hoo! Would you look at that?" Beth Ann said. "Stand around and keep talking, boys, I'll fish. I just got the first one, and he's a whopper. I believe you owe me the biggest one caught today, unless you want to give me the extras after we divide them up."

She landed the first catfish easily. The boys hurried to get their lines in the river. They didn't want to be outdone by a girl, even if it was Beth Ann.

****

"You mean we actually have to spend the night at Granny Rose's while we're working this case?" Daniel said.

"It's not like any of us would be alone," Hank said. "She's got a big place; and it will take all of us to help out. Besides, I think Abraham would appreciate the company. Like Deputy Collins said, it's too big a job for him to do alone. Granny can't help out much while she's recovering."

"But we *have* to stay all night with her? In her *house*? With *her* in the next room?" Daniel said. "Please tell me you're just messing with me, Hank. You know how I feel about that old woman."

"What better way to get to know her and find out for yourself that she's a sweet old lady," Beth Ann said. "Are you sure she won't get suspicious of our being there, Hank?"

"I'll have the deputy tell her we're just there to help Abraham. I'll suggest we stay with her overnight to make sure we can get an early start every morning."

"How long are we talking about being there?" Beth Ann said.

"How long do you think we'll need to be there?" Hank said.

"Don't ask me. I don't want to be there at all," Daniel said.

"How long do you think your dad will let you stay with her, Beth Ann?"

"I'm not sure, but I think he'll let me stay a couple of days, especially since I'll be helping her out around the house. He might let me stay a week."

"Where are you suggesting we sleep, Hank?"

"*When* we sleep, you and I will need to stay in the barn, where Abraham stays. Beth Ann will be in the house."

"What do you mean *when*?" Daniel said. "I'm not like you, Hank. I *need* my sleep."

"The three of us will take turns keeping watch. We don't want to be caught off-guard should Pinky and his night friends show up unexpected."

"What about me, Hank?" Jimmy Jack said.

"We need you to stay around our place. Someone's got to keep watch there. You need to listen to what Ma and Deputy Collins talk about, too. If they say something that could help us, you've got to let us know. I'll be coming home to do my chores when I can. You can report anything that might be important to me then."

Jimmy Jack sat a little taller on the rock and smiled.

"I can do that," he said. "Thanks, Hank, for letting me help you guys. I really like doing things with you. This is going to be fun."

"It's not a game, Jimmy Jack." Hank said. "We'll be depending on you to keep us informed."

"I won't let you down. I promised, remember?"

"Okay. Beth Ann, do you understand what to do?"

"I'll ask my dad about anybody he may have treated during the night recently. Then we can see if there's a connection to the glow in the sky."

"He won't get suspicious of your questions, will he?" Daniel said.

"No, he knows I want to be a doctor. I'm always asking him about how to do medical stuff. He'd be more suspicious if I *didn't* ask him questions."

"Don't forget to ask him about helping Granny Rose out and how to be his assistant while you're there," Hank said.

"I won't."

"Daniel, do you understand your job?"

"Yeah, I just need to be my nosy self in town and find out what kind of stuff goes on at night. Maybe we'll get lucky and be able to identify the weird activity in the woods you keep seeing. You're sure you aren't just imagining things?"

"I'm not imagining anything. Deputy Collins heard and saw the same thing I did just last night."

"Okay. I'll try to find out if there is anything going on at Beech Hill, too. I just hope it's nothing like what happened at Cross Roads a couple of months ago. You remember when those roughnecks from the oil fields caused a ruckus there?"

"Yeah, I hope that's not happening at Beech Hill, too," Hank said. "Let's meet in our loft at the end of the week. We can decide then if our plan to be at Granny Rose's is ready to go. Come on, Jimmy Jack. We need to get home before supper."

"Wait up, Hank," Beth Ann said. "I need to ask you something."

"Go on, Jimmy Jack. I'll be right behind you."

As soon as Jimmy Jack was safely out of earshot but still visible, Daniel joined Beth Ann and Hank on the trail.

"Are you sure you shouldn't tell Deputy Collins? I mean, Granny Rose is his family. I think, that is, Daniel and I think he has a right to know what's going on."

Beth Ann's serious tone alarmed Hank. Daniel nodded, the wrinkles between his brows deep.

"Don't you understand? If I tell him and he gets hurt, I'll be the one to blame."

"Hank, we're missing something here," Beth Ann said. "What aren't you telling us?"

"I've got to go. I'll see you in a few days."

CHAPTER 6

A SCREECH OWL IN THE sweet gum tree outside Hank's open window woke him from a deep sleep. He sat straight up in bed; the hard pounding of his heart practically bruised his chest. He heard it fly off; then he lay back down, wide awake. The crickets, cicadas, and frogs combined their noisy songs in a prayer for rain, keeping him awake. Hank went to the window to shut out the noise. Just before he turned to go back to bed, his eye caught a large shadowy figure go into the woods along the trail to the fishing hole. It was lightning fast. One second it was there; the next it was gone. He leaned way out the window to get a better look. *Where did it go?* It was too far away to hear anything. The clock in the sitting room softly chimed twice. *Forget about it, Hank. You've got enough to keep you busy right now. It's probably some bootlegger, anyway, trying to scare off the competition.*

Hank turned away from the window and tried to go back to sleep. He wondered how so many noises that fade or are silent in the daylight could be so loud at night. Besides the noises outside, he heard the clock ticking from the sitting room as if it were in his room. Then there were the pops and creaks from the house settling. Jimmy Jack's breathing and talking in his sleep kept him awake, too. In frustration, he turned onto his back and cradled his head in his hands, staring at the ceiling.

His mind recalled the images of his ma and the deputy as he kissed her cheek, as she held his hands, and as they hugged. He thought about those images and realized he wasn't as disturbed by them as he thought he'd be. He was glad his ma had someone besides him and Jimmy Jack to care for. He reached for the framed medal on the table beside his bed. Ma had let him keep the glass off the frame so he could touch the medal whenever he wanted. He fingered the details of the ribbon and star, seeing them clearly in his mind. It brought comfort when he thought about the good times he had spent with his father before he left for the war. There seemed to be something different this time, though. Instead of thinking of his father, Hank thought about Deputy Collins. An undeniable peace about his presence in the family washed over him.

Hank contemplated his feelings about the deputy while fingering the medal. He wasn't so unlike his father. They shared a lot of similarities, both physically and in their principles; but they had their differences, too. They were individuals who shared qualities that Hank couldn't deny. How many times had Hank mistaken the deputy for his father in the past several weeks? Was it just last night or the night before that he had confused their voices at the cemetery? In the heat of the fight on Sunday, he couldn't decide if he was seeing and hearing his father or someone else. He thought about what Deputy Collins had said that afternoon.

"If something happens to you or your family, how do you think I would feel, especially if I could have prevented it if you had told me?"

Hank remembered the conversation they had had before leaving the cemetery.

"Did you hear and see that in the woods just now?" Hank said.

"Yeah, I need to get you home so I can check it out."

"I'll be all right. Go on. I'll get home okay."

"Are you crazy? Your ma would have my hide if she knew I had found you and let you do that, especially with all that's happened."

"I won't tell if you won't."

"That's not the way it works, Hank. Not when you love someone. You don't keep secrets from those you love."

Hank returned the framed medal to its place, then turned away from the window and closed his eyes.

"Hank, get up, son," Ma said.

Hank opened his eyes to the brightness of a lantern. *Did I really go back to sleep?* His squinting eyes burned till they adjusted to the light. He looked around, bewildered.

"What's wrong, Ma."

Jimmy Jack sat up in his bed on the other side of the room.

"Ma? What's that smell?" he said.

Hank smelled the smoke, too.

"Something's on fire outside. Hank, I need you to get dressed and meet me on the back porch. Hurry, now."

Hank didn't hesitate. When he got to the back porch, Ma was looking in the direction of Granny Rose's farm. There was thick smoke rising above the trees in the predawn light.

"I need you to get to Granny Rose's as fast as you can. I don't think it's her house burning, but it could be her crops. She'll need help putting it out."

"Yes, ma'am. What about Deputy Collins? Who's going to get him?"

"He's probably already there. Go on, son. Help them."

Hank heard the sob in her voice and saw her tears.

"Don't worry, Ma. I'm going right now."

Hank leaped off the back porch and ran faster than he thought possible. He took the shortcut, taking the trail through the woods behind the chicken yard and barn on the Baker property. When he broke through the tree line at the backside of Granny's cornfield a few minutes later, he saw the flames. Abraham and Deputy Collins ran toward the fire with buckets dripping from the pump in the backyard. Hank ran to the storage shed and grabbed the shovel. He caught a glimpse of Granny as she watched from the screened-in back porch. She nodded at him, then he took the shovel to Deputy Collins.

"Here, I'll take over for you."

"Thanks. You and Abraham keep the water coming as fast as you can. I'll start digging over there before it reaches the woods."

Hank ran for more water and saw lights from a couple of motor cars turning onto Granny's property. Several men got out and pulled shovels from the backs of both vehicles. Four men surrounded the flames, digging trenches around the field. Three strangers joined him and Abraham with their own buckets. He recognized Sheriff Stan, Mr. Milner, Doc Warden, and Mr. Wagner. Hank's heart swelled with pride in the Farmville citizens that didn't hesitate to help when there was a need. *Are we all breaking the law, Pinky? Helping a neighbor save her corn crop? Working alongside Abraham, fighting flames and destruction?*

****

It took a couple of hours to make sure the fire was completely out. The sun was well above the trees when Deputy Collins shook hands with the men who had helped. They all turned toward the house at the sweet sound of the giant triangle, announcing breakfast. Hank looked around at Abraham and the others. *We all look alike.* Dirt mixed with the sweat on their faces, arms, and hands. Hank couldn't help smiling.

"Come on, everybody," Deputy Collins said. "Let's get washed up for breakfast. We'd best not keep the women waiting too long."

"Abraham, what's wrong?" Hank said, alarmed at his friend's posture.

Abraham had collapsed to his knees and buried his face in his hands. Hank knelt beside him and put an arm around the boy's shuddering shoulders.

"It's okay, Abraham. We got it out. Let's go get some food. I'm starving. Nothing like putting in a full day's work before breakfast, wouldn't you say?"

Abraham maintained a prayerful position. He raised his face toward heaven with his eyes closed.

"Hank, I was so scared. I'm still shaking. I don't think I can stand."

"Come on," Hank said. "Let me help you."

He helped Abraham stand and supported him, putting one of his friend's heavy arms around his own shoulders. He staggered under the extra weight until Deputy Collins came alongside and put Abraham's other arm around his shoulders. Together they helped the exhausted boy to the house. *How long were Abraham and Deputy Collins fighting that fire alone? Wait a minute. How did the men from town know Granny Rose needed help?*

****

Ma had created a feast for the men who helped save Granny's farm. The aroma of fresh bacon, fried eggs, and biscuits made from scratch couldn't totally replace the smell of smoke; but Hank's growling stomach didn't care. He hadn't realized how hungry he was till he sat down at the table. Every bite exploded with flavor. Hank looked at the people around the room and smiled. No one cared that they were eating at the same table with Abraham. He belonged. He was family. Deputy Collins kept filling the boy's plate when it was nearly empty. As his own hunger was satisfied, Hank wondered if Pinky was making good on his threat. There was no time to waste. His plan couldn't wait.

"What's going to happen, now?" Hank said.

"I'm starting an investigation, as soon as I can, to figure out who set that fire," Deputy Collins said.

"What about Granny Rose and Abraham? What will happen to them?"

"I wish you people would stop talking about me like I'm not here. I'm fine. Better than fine. I can take care of myself and that boy, too. Don't you worry about Abraham and me, Hank; we'll be okay. I should have had my shotgun handy."

"Did you see who did this, Granny?" Deputy Collins said.

Granny placed fresh biscuits from the oven on the table.

"No, but I have an idea. I didn't take him as seriously as I should have the other day, but he won't make a fool of me again."

"Were you threatened?" the deputy said. "Who threatened you? Let me and the sheriff handle this, Granny. You don't need to bring on another heart attack."

"Now, you listen here, Peter James Collins..."

Hank couldn't help snickering. He stopped abruptly when the deputy gave him the look that didn't need defining.

"...I haven't lived this long by having someone else fight my battles. Your mama and daddy learned early on to let me take care of myself without any outside help; and he was a lawman, too. I don't need anyone getting hurt on my account. And don't think I can't handle this myself. You take care of your investigation if you think you need to. File the paperwork Stan, there, needs to keep it legal. When the time comes, stay out of my way, boy. This is my fight, not yours."

Guilt demanded satisfaction from Hank. It was time to act.

"Ma, if it's okay with you and Deputy Collins, and Granny, of course, I'd like to stay here. I can help Abraham with running the farm while Granny rests up. I think Daniel and Beth Ann would be willing to help, too. We wouldn't be any trouble, Granny. I promise. All we'll do is help with the chores and anything else you say needs to be done. Daniel and I will sleep in the barn with Abraham, and Beth Ann can stay with you in the house. It would only be for a few days, till you get back on your feet. Will you please let us help you?"

CHAPTER 7

ALL WAS STILL, AS IF frozen in time, for several seconds. The light over the table buzzed, breaking the silence along with the ticking clock on the wall. Ma and the deputy clasped hands. She smiled and nodded. Granny slowly and quietly stacked dirty plates from around the table.

"Granny?" Deputy Collins said.

"What do you say, Granny?" Hank said. "I can get Daniel to help me with the chores today, if it's all right with Mr. Wagner. Abraham is really tired. I'll bet Beth Ann would help out around the house, too, with your permission, Dr. Warden. I could be back here with them both within an hour. You won't even have to pay us. We'll do it for free."

Hank watched Granny quickly grab a dishtowel from the countertop, hiding shaking hands. They made eye contact briefly. He almost missed the slight smile she gave him.

"I think the boy's got a good idea," Dr. Warden said. "What do you think, Wagner? Could your boy help Hank and Abraham with the farm while my Beth Ann lent a hand in the house?"

"If Granny Rose doesn't mind, I'd be proud to have my boy put in some time around here," Mr. Wagner said. "What do you say, Granny? It's your decision."

Hank's eyes pleaded with the old woman.

"Granny, think about it. Please," Pete said, as he took her hands in his. "Stan gave me the day off, but I really want to get started on my investigation as soon as I get cleaned up. I'd feel better knowing you and Abraham weren't alone out here."

Granny turned to the sink, leaned against it, closed her eyes, and bowed her head, resting her chin on her chest.

"Go ahead, boy, go get your friends. You all can stay till the end of the week. I'm much obliged, Dr. Warden and Mr. Wagner, for your offer. Miss Martha, you have a fine boy, there. He's a lot like his daddy, helping out when he can where he can. Let me make myself perfectly clear, though, about what I said earlier. I will handle this myself. I won't put your children in danger. Don't get in my way, any of you, or try to stop me. I mean to tend to this mess on my own terms. I won't have anyone getting hurt on my account or out of ignorance." Hank saw her grimace. When she spoke again, he was relieved; but he watched her movements carefully, sensing something wasn't right.

"Pete, you go do what it is you think you need to do. I won't stop you. Just be careful. The ones who did this may be sly, but they aren't smart. They'll be back, and I'll be ready for them. I'd like to thank the rest of you for helping out this morning. You're welcome to…"

When Granny grimaced, again, she grabbed her left shoulder, her face pale, and collapsed.

"Dr. Warden," Hank said, frantic to get to her before anyone else.

Everyone at the table gathered around her. She looked as if she were sleeping.

"Give her some air, men," Dr. Warden said.

Hank cradled her head in his lap. Pete held her small hands in one large hand and caressed her cheek with the back of the other. Hank's eyes pleaded with the deputy's, his tears dropping into her hair.

"Don't let her die, Mr. Pete," Hank said.

Pete put a warm hand on Hank's shoulder and gently squeezed.

"Let's get her to bed," Dr. Warden said.

* * * * * * *

It was just before sundown when Abraham, Hank, and Daniel finished with all the chores around the farm. They were putting the chickens to bed when Beth Ann rang the triangle for dinner.

"Hank, Daniel, I'm truly grateful for your help today. Go on to the house. I'll shut up the chickens," Abraham said.

"Are you sure?" Hank said. "You still don't look too good."

"Yeah. See you at the house."

"Don't be long. I'm hungry enough to eat a horse."

"I'm too tired to eat," Daniel said as they walked slowly toward the house.

"You'll get hungry before morning if you don't."

"I don't care. I just want to go home and go to bed."

Hank stepped in front of Daniel, grabbing his upper arms to stop him.

"Go home? Didn't your daddy tell you we were staying the night?"

"What? Uh-uh! I'm not staying out here with a crazy woman."

"She's not crazy. She's sick and needs our help."

"How do you know she's not just joshing all of us? She can't be sick. She's not normal like everyone else."

"Suit yourself. I'm staying," Hank said, resuming the walk to the house. "How are you getting home?"

"I thought your ma was picking us up." Daniel ran to catch up.

"Nope."

"Deputy Collins?"

"Uh-uh. He's camping out in the woods. He thinks he has a good chance of catching whoever set the fire if they don't know he's around."

"Well, I'm way too tired to walk home."

"Then I guess you're staying." Hank giggled.

"Oh, man. You're enjoying this, aren't you?"

"Come on, Daniel. It'll be fun sleeping in the barn. Abraham says it's just like being at home."

"Yeah, well, that tells me he's already under Granny's spell. How do you know we won't be after spending a night here?"

"I tell you what, if we *are* under a spell in the morning, I'll say I'm sorry, okay?" Hank couldn't help laughing out loud.

"This isn't funny, Hank. That woman scares me. I guess she's never shown you her evil eye. That's how she casts her spells, you know. But I didn't give her the chance to finish her spell on me. Why else do you think I listen in church? It only took one look to know she had me in her sights." Daniel shuddered.

"When did she do that?"

"When I was five."

"What?" Hank giggled, again. "You've been scared of her all because of a look she gave you at church when you were five? I'll bet you were noisy or something and kept her from hearing the preacher. She doesn't have an evil eye. Besides, don't you think church is the last place she'd be casting spells?"

"I'm telling you, Hank. She's got everyone fooled around here. She's evil."

"And I suppose Deputy Collins is evil, too, because he's her grandson?"

"It's a thought."

As they climbed the steps to the house, Hank draped his arm around Daniel's sagging shoulders.

"Have you been reading those spooky books, again? Man, you need to stick to Sherlock Holmes."

* * * * * * *

Hank took the first watch from the loft. All was quiet except for Daniel's light snoring. He kept nodding off until he heard distant gunfire. *Wake up, Hank. Everyone's depending on you to be on lookout.* Hank sat on the window frame and thought about Pinky's threats and the fire. *It's too much of a coincidence to not be connected.* Someone stirred behind him as he watched the tree line for anything unusual. Nothing. Then it was there.

Hank slowly stood and leaned out the window. A big shadow had appeared at the edge of the woods. It looked like a man, but he couldn't be sure. It was definitely large. *What is that, and what's it looking at?* The back of his neck tingled, and the hair stood straight up. *I wonder if Deputy Collins can see it.* He looked at the sky above the trees. Nothing. When he looked back at the tree line, it was gone. Vanished. Someone touched his shoulder. He swung around and smacked Abraham in the jaw with his fist, knocking him on his backside.

"It's just me, Hank," Abraham said. He rubbed his jaw and worked it gingerly.

Sweat beaded on Hank's upper lip and along his hairline. Electric impulses charged every nerve along his spine.

"Abraham, I'm sorry. I didn't hear you."

Hank helped his friend stand.

"What spooked you out there?"

"I don't know. Maybe nothing." He turned back to the window, searching the trees, again. "I…"

He squinted his eyes, trying to focus on the trees nearest the burned cornfield.

"What?" Abraham said, joining Hank at the window, watching.

"I keep…"

He turned away from the window, thoughtful.

"You keep what?"

"I keep seeing this…thing out near the trees."

The bright moon allowed Hank to see the whites of Abraham's eyes shine all around his dark brown irises.

"It's probably nothing. I'm just tired."

Abraham relaxed and nodded. "Go get some sleep. I'll take over."

He leaned way out the window, checking the woods for several seconds before he finally relaxed against the windowsill. Hank sat back against the wall beside the window, too worked up to sleep, and watched Abraham's face closely. He sensed more than fatigue from his friend.

"Are you all right, Abraham?"

"Why do you ask?"

"You're not just tired, are you?"

Abraham was silent for several seconds before answering.

"I guess not. I've been thinking about things."

"What kind of things?"

Abraham took a long, slow breath. "I'm not sure it was such a good idea to stay here."

"Why not?" Hank stood, heartbreaking jolts pulsed through his veins at the thought of his friend leaving. "Is that why you were so upset this morning? Are you blaming yourself for the fire?"

"What if I am?"

"Well, stop it. No one's blaming you. Did someone accuse you of starting it?"

Abraham took another deep breath.

"No, but…"

Hank put a hand on his friend's shoulder.

"Then why beat yourself up over something that wasn't your doing?"

"It may not have been my doing, but it *was* my fault."

"Now, that makes about as much sense as me being responsible for my daddy going to war and getting himself killed." Hank was surprised at his words.

"You don't understand, Hank. You can't understand. You're white."

"What's color got to do with it?"

Abraham looked at Hank intently.

"What?"

"You really don't see my skin color, do you? Not everybody's like you, Hank."

"Then help me understand."

CHAPTER 8

"I DON'T KNOW HIS NAME," Abraham said, sitting with Hank under the window, again. "I saw him with Granny the other day when we went to Snow Hill. He had her backed into a corner at Palmer's Grocery Store. They had words, but I was too far away to hear what they said. As soon as I realized she was in trouble, I went right over to help her. She stomped his foot before I could get to them. He raised his hand to hit her, but I stopped him before he could touch her. Then the sheriff walked in." He paused, shaking his head.

"He was just a kid like you and me, but there was so much hate in his green eyes. I truly believe he would have killed me right then and there if the sheriff hadn't been standing at the counter. Just before he walked away, he told Granny that if she won't take care of 'this here mangy, stray dog,' then he would with *great* pleasure. That's when I knew they'd been arguing about me."

"Green eyes. Was he a chubby kid with red hair? A little older than me and tall?"

"Yeah, do you know him?"

"We've had a few run-ins. His name's Pinky McLeod. Did you see him this morning?"

"I can't be sure. It was too dark."

"Why didn't you tell Deputy Collins or Sheriff Stan?"

Abraham stood up to look out the window. "The deputy's got enough to worry about, what with Granny's health and all. If I leave, there won't be any need to get the law involved. Her problems will be gone."

"Abraham, you can't leave. Granny needs you. Besides, where would you go?"

"I don't know. Maybe north."

"If you let Pinky McLeod and his kind scare you off, when does it stop? What about your family? Do they know?"

"No. They're fine right where they are at Beech Hill. I've never seen Mammy so happy. I don't need to bring trouble to them, too."

Hank stood beside Abraham. "People, like Pinky, don't just pick on one person at a time. If skin color is his only reason to hate you, what makes you so sure your family isn't being bullied, too?"

"They can take care of themselves. It wouldn't be the first time. Hank, I really don't like fighting."

"Sometimes you have to. Daddy used to tell me not to start fights. But there's a difference in starting a fight and defending yourself."

"I couldn't live with myself if I caused something terrible to happen to Granny, you, or anybody else I cared about."

Anger ignited Hank's words. "So you're going to let that bully, an ignorant white boy, rob you of the best thing you've had in your life, right here in Farmville, because of your skin color? What about your neighbors? Those men who fought that fire right alongside you this morning don't care what color you are. They sat at the same table and ate breakfast with you, Abraham. Didn't you hear Granny? She's not backing down, even with a bad heart. Are you going to throw away all she's done, all she's doing, for you?"

"That's not fair, Hank."

"Oh, really. What's not fair, Abraham? Do you actually think Pinky will leave Granny Rose alone just because you leave? Think again. The threats won't magically go away with you. *That's* what's not fair. She's willing to risk her life because she's your friend. Beth Ann, Daniel, and I don't care what color you are, either. You're our friend first. If that doesn't matter to you, then go ahead and leave."

"I won't let any of you get hurt on my account. I don't have a choice."

Hank heard his friend's anger, and pushed his own anger away.

"You've always got a choice, Abraham. We all do."

"Now who's being unrealistic? Colored people don't have choices. We don't have rights like you white folks do."

"Then let's change that. But what changes if you go? You'll always be running."

"How can my staying bring the changes that need to happen, Hank?"

"I don't know, but it has to."

"You're dreaming if you really think my being here will make things better."

"How long will you give me to prove it?"

Daniel stirred in his bunk. "Will you two be quiet so I can sleep?"

"Abraham wants to leave, Daniel. We've got to stop him."

Daniel yawned and rubbed his eyes.

"It's Granny Rose, isn't it? I told you she was evil, Hank."

"Stop it, Daniel."

"It's not Granny," Abraham said. "I have other reasons."

"Give us till Sunday to prove your reasons stink. Daniel, Beth Ann, and I are looking into some things that will help you see you're wrong."

"Uh, Hank," Daniel said, sitting up and scratching his head. "I don't think that'll be enough time."

"What do you say, Abraham? Will you give us till Sunday?"

"What if you're *wrong*, Hank?"

"What if we're not?"

Daniel fell back onto the pallet with a huff. "Guys, can we *please* talk about this in the morning? I really need to sleep."

"You've got till Sunday."

Hank nodded, satisfied.

* * * * * * *

Hank was determined to keep the mood around the breakfast table light. It was impossible to miss Abraham's lack of appetite while Daniel worked on his fourth plate of scrambled eggs, grits, and bacon. Hank avoided Beth Ann's eyes and her attempt to read his face while she refilled Daniel's plate, yet again. He was relieved when Granny shuffled into the room, welcoming the distraction.

"Are you sure you should be up, Granny?" Hank said, using his best "Deputy Collins" impression. "What would Doc say if he were here?"

He noticed she looked better after a good night's sleep, and was glad to see some color back in her face. He heard several snickers around the kitchen as she wagged her finger at him.

"I'm the best judge of how I feel, young man. Eat and mind your own business."

Granny sat while Beth Ann took the buttermilk biscuits out of the oven. The aroma of crispy bacon and coffee filled the house. Without warning, someone walked heavily across the back porch. Hank's heart stopped until he saw Deputy Collins walk through the door.

"Something smells good in here," he said.

"Take a seat, Deputy," Beth Ann said. "How do you like your eggs?"

"Sunny side up, Miss Warden. I'll have two, if you please."

He leaned over and kissed Granny's cheek.

"Shouldn't you be in bed, Granny," the deputy said.

Granny swatted him with her flyswatter on his backside. They chuckled when they hugged. Hank smiled.

"Sit down and have some breakfast, boy."

"I need to clean up, first. Hold off on those eggs, Beth Ann. I won't be long."

"Yes, sir."

"Hey, Deputy, can I talk to you a moment…alone?" Hank said.

"Sure, walk with me."

Hank scraped his chair away from the table, took one last swallow of milk, and followed the deputy to the back bedroom.

"What's on your mind?" Deputy Collins took off his shirt before pouring water in the basin. He washed up quickly then put on a clean shirt from the bureau.

"Granny said she needed to go to Snow Hill today, but she really should take it easy and stay close to home. I was thinking that Daniel and I could go for her. Abraham could stay and watch after things here, so Granny and Beth Ann aren't alone."

"That's a good idea. Put the bill on my account. Did she give you a list?"

"Not yet. I wanted to check with you first, in case you already had plans to go yourself."

"Actually, I'm following some leads and don't have time to go. It would be a big help to me if you would take care of it. Tell Mr. Palmer I'll be by in a day or two to pay the bill. Thanks, Hank. You're showing real maturity with this whole situation. I'm proud of you. I think your dad would be, too."

Hank hadn't realized his muscles were tensed until he turned to leave.

"One more thing."

Hank froze just inside the doorway, holding his breath. *He knows something.*

"Toby's been favoring his right foreleg. Keep an eye on it, will you?"

He swallowed the fear that shook his insides, forcing his breathing to look normal.

"Sure."

"Come on, now. Breakfast smells really good. Don't want to keep the cook waiting too long."

* * * * * * *

Hank reined in Toby to a stop before turning the wagon onto the main street in Snow Hill. He and Daniel watched a muscular colored man handle a team of eight oxen pulling logs toward Miller's Bluff.

"Where's the snow?" Daniel said.

Hank nodded toward a large group of tents that he guessed spread out over at least three acres of land, if not five or more.

"Maybe *that's* why it's called Snow Hill."

The white canvases made the ground look snow-covered. Not far from the tents, wood buildings lined both sides of the main street. There were signs for the hotel, a theater, a drug store, a church, and some other buildings. Hank stopped the wagon in front of Palmer's Grocery Store.

"This is it," he said.

"This is where Abraham saw Pinky?" Daniel said.

"Yep."

Hank retrieved the list from his shirt pocket.

"Let's get to work. I'll get the order filled. You sniff out the clues, Mr. Holmes."

"If there's anything we can use to help Abraham and Granny here, I'll find it."

They jumped down from the wagon at the same time on opposite sides.

Hank watched his best friend enter the store. He admired Daniel's "Sherlock Holmes" abilities. He told Hank the key was to be a good listener and know when to ask the right questions. Hank thought about how Daniel could go just about anywhere anytime and learn anything about anybody *without* raising suspicions. He was always full of news and information about the goings on in Farmville. Hank wished he could be as carefree as Daniel was. He was a kid without a care in the world, except for Granny Rose. Not Hank, he was the man of the house and had been since the day his daddy left for the war. There was no hope of having what Daniel had, now. *Stop. This isn't the time or place to feel sorry for yourself. Get your mind on why we're here.*

After tying Toby to the hitching post, Hank looked over Granny's list as he entered the store and stepped up to the counter.

"What can I do for you, young man?"

"I need to pick up these things for a friend." He handed the gentleman the list. "Deputy Collins said to put the bill on his account."

"Let me guess—Granny Rose?"

Hank smiled.

"You know her?"

"Sure do. Fine lady. I heard she wasn't feeling well lately. Give her my best, will you?"

How did he know she was sick? Hank pushed his suspicions to the back of his mind. *He's just being friendly, for goodness sake. What's your problem, Hank?*

"I'll tell her."

"I'll be right back with these things. Feel free to have a look around."

"Thanks. I'll just wait here."

The bell above the door jangled. Hank immediately took cover behind a nearby shelf, carefully peeking around the corner. Pinky McLeod walked through the door with a couple of boys who looked to be about his age or older. He tossed each of his friends a peach before he picked out a couple of plums, putting one in his shirt pocket and eating the other.

"Hey, you've got to pay for that," the clerk said.

"Yeah, yeah, Pops," Pinky said. "I'm good for it. Come on, guys, there's nothing else in here we want."

"You get back here and pay for that fruit."

The boys laughed as they ran across the street. Hank looked for Daniel. He was talking with a tall, blond-haired boy at the back of the store. The clerk returned to the counter with a box filled with various items from the list.

"Here you go, son. Sorry about the scene. That boy's nothing but trouble. You'll have to go to the drug store for the rest. It's just up the street to your left. Can't miss it."

Hank picked up the box and took the list from the clerk.

"Thank you, sir. Deputy Collins said to tell you he'd pay the bill in a day or two."

"That's fine. Tell him not to worry."

Hank waited for Daniel at the wagon. He checked the mule's leg. Then he rubbed Toby's nose and gave him a carrot from the box, deep in thought. He nearly jumped clean out of his skin when Daniel called out. Every nerve was on edge after seeing Pinky. The blond-haired boy Daniel had been with in the store was right behind him.

"Not so loud, Daniel," Hank and the blond-haired boy said in unison.

"This is Charlie."

CHAPTER 9

"You were right," Daniel said. "Charlie, here, knows about some pretty bad stuff that's going on out at Beech Hill."

"What kind of stuff," Hank said.

"Tell him, Charlie."

"Yeah, a group of five or six guys dress up in white sheets and hoods and ride out on horses to Beech Hill every now and then in the middle of the night."

"Why Beech Hill?" Hank said.

"Don't you know? It's one of the fastest growing colored towns around these here parts. These riders usually have a particular family or someone they mean to put the 'fear of God' into already singled out." Charlie put his hands in his pockets and kicked at rocks in the dirt. Hank noticed the boy wouldn't make eye contact with him. "They all have guns, torches, and rope to pull down sheds, tents, and anything else they want gone. They make good and sure everyone knows they're there to pass judgment. Then they burn a cross in the yard while the whole community, children and all, watch. They'll also run off the livestock that's corralled and tar and feather anyone who tries to stop them or gets in their way. I can't get the looks on those poor people's faces out of my head. It keeps me awake at night. It's like they're looking at demons in the flesh or something. It's awful."

"How do you know about this? Have you seen it yourself?" Hank said.

"Yeah." Charlie looked at Hank briefly. "My brother is one of the raiders. I got curious and followed him a couple of times, to see what he was doing."

"Why haven't you told your dad?" Daniel said.

"I can't." Hank watched the boy's face when he looked at Daniel as if he were crazy for asking such a question. Then the boy leaned back, relaxed against the hitching post, and crossed his arms over his chest. "He's the one who got it all started. He asked some fellows from Little Rock to help him get rid of the Beech Hill settlement because it's growing too fast. He's afraid of another situation happening here, like what took place a couple of months ago out at Cross Roads. As long as the colored people don't try to get jobs in the oilfields other than teamsters, it's tolerable. But some of the men from Beech Hill are trying to get work as roustabouts. My dad is scared it will cause a worse problem with government interference than the trouble at Cross Roads did. He's proud my brother rides with them. What worries me is the raids are getting more violent. I'm afraid someone's going to get hurt or killed, maybe even my brother."

"How do you know when they are planning a raid?" Hank said.

Charlie waited for a wagon to pass the store on the street before answering. He made steady eye contact with Hank for the first time. "They have a secret meeting to set things in motion. Then a day or two after the raid, there's a general town meeting to discuss what happened and how to manage it. These men from Little Rock don't tell the people what the raiders are doing. They're just making it look like the town's in danger, and they're scaring everybody into accepting their solutions without questions."

"Do you think these raids are what the glowing skies are about, Hank?"

"Yeah, sounds like it could be. When's the next meeting, Charlie? I want to listen in on it."

"Tonight. It's after sundown. Only a few know it's happening. That's how they operate. They'll be meeting at the church, so no one suspects anything if they *are* seen."

"Hey, Hutch. Where's my money?" Pinky said.

All three jumped at the familiar voice coming from across the street, unaware of his close proximity. Charlie and Daniel stared wide-eyed as Pinky and his two friends stepped up to the wagon and looked over the sides. Hank stayed out of Pinky's sight, behind the mule's big head, for the moment.

"I've told you I don't owe you any money," Charlie said.

"And I say you do. If it weren't for me, you'd have been caught the other night. There's no telling what those guys would have done to a *spy*. Isn't that right, boys? Who's your little friend, there?" Pinky said. "Hey, you aren't from Snow Hill. Didn't I see you at that church in Farmville Sunday?"

All Daniel could do was stare with his mouth open and nod.

"You'd better shut your mouth before you let flies in." Pinky and his friends chuckled. "Where's that *mama's boy* friend of yours? Is *Henry Stuart* still crying or is he just yellow like his old man, scared of running into me again?"

"Why would *I* be afraid of *you*?" Hank said, stepping out from behind Toby. He stood between Daniel and Charlie. For an instant, Hank saw fear on Pinky's face and in his eyes, sweat beaded his upper lip.

"Where'd you get that black eye, huh?" Hank said. "Why Pinky, I believe you're turning pale, or is that yellow?"

Pinky looked up and down the busy street.

"Come on, guys. Let's get out of here." He pointed at Hank then at Charlie. "I'll deal with you later, farm boy. I want my money for saving your scrawny hide last week, Charlie Hutch. I'll give you till tomorrow to get it, or you'll *wish* you had."

"Why the rush, Pinky? No one to get me off you this time?"

"Hank, what are you doing?"

"Oh, don't worry, Daniel. He's all bark and no bite, anyway."

"We'll see who's still standing the next time I see you, Baker." Pinky walked backward across the street from where he'd come, watching Hank till he almost tripped on the boardwalk. "You'd better keep a watch over your shoulders. I'm coming for you… soon."

"Ooo, I'm so scared I'm shaking all over."

"You may not be, but I am," Daniel said.

"He's trouble, Hank," Charlie said. "He and those two with him were part of the last raid my brother went on."

Daniel's face paled as he looked from Hank to Charlie and back to Hank.

"What do you suppose he meant by 'coming for you'?" Daniel said.

"Most likely, he's planning a raid on *your* place like the ones at Beech Hill," Charlie said. "If it's not already planned, it will be. I've heard my brother talk about how you and an old woman helped a colored family move here. He wasn't real happy about it, either."

"Are all their raids at night?" Hank said.

"Yeah. They're usually either really late or just before dawn, when they can strike the most fear."

Hank contemplated his next words carefully before speaking.

"Why are you telling us all of this? Are you friend or foe, Charlie? Did you take part in those raids?"

"What?"

"No, it's all right, Daniel," Charlie said. "He's asking good questions. I don't like how fast Beech Hill is growing any more than my dad does. But the fact is, I don't like what my brother is doing even more."

"What was Pinky talking about when he called you a spy?" Daniel said.

"He saw me watching them on the last raid before I could hide. He knows I won't go to the sheriff because of my brother, but he wants money to keep *his* mouth shut. I've seen what those guys do to anyone who tries to stop them. But I really don't think my brother would let them do anything to me. Giving Pinky money won't stop him, though. I know he'll keep coming back for more because it's easy. That's how he gets money. I won't give him that satisfaction."

"You still haven't told us why you're telling us all of this," Hank said.

"I have to tell someone. Why not someone who can help me stop what's happening before someone gets killed?"

"I want to be at the meeting tonight. Where can we meet so we can both be there?"

"Hank, you're not serious, are you? How are you going to get here?"

"That'll be my worry, Daniel."

"You have to be here around sundown. I'll be waiting for you in the woods behind Palmer's Grocery Store."

"Come on, Daniel. We've got a few more things to get before going back. I'll see you around sundown, Charlie."

* * * * * * *

Hank tied Toby to a tree branch in the woods behind Palmer's Grocery Store. It was hard to make out some things in the light of dusk. A whip-o-will called from the top of the tree he used for a hitching post. In the distance another whip-o-will returned the call. The fluttering of a bird in flight and the chirping of crickets and cicadas added their cadences to Hank's heartbeats as the adrenaline rushed through his veins. He made out Charlie's shadow before he left the darkness of the woods. Hank used his imitation of an owl's call to alert Charlie to his presence. He turned and watched Hank quickly and carefully bound from the woods to the back porch of the store.

"We need to stay here till they're all inside the church. We can watch them from here, then sneak to the window," Charlie said.

"How long will we have to wait?"

"They'll start gathering real soon."

The boys quietly watched from the shadows of the building. With clouds overhead, the moon couldn't light the path to the church. Hank was glad Charlie was there to lead the way. Without warning, a light shone through one of the windows at the back of the church.

"Did you see anyone go inside?" Hank said. He could understand the fear their victims had when these men were like ghosts that just appear out of nowhere.

"No, but that's not unusual. They come from the woods and move with the shadows so no one knows they're there."

"When do we go?"

"Not for a few minutes. We don't want to risk being seen. It could get ugly if that happened. We'd be forced to take part or they'd make sure we couldn't interfere. We'll give them a couple more minutes, then we'll go."

The wait was nerve-wracking. Hank's heel wouldn't stop bobbing. He had learned to keep moving so his muscles didn't cramp, but this wait was longer than he was used to.

"Let's go," Charlie said. "Keep your head down and try not to make any noise."

They quickly ran between buildings after making sure no one was about. They pressed against the walls and blended into the shadows, moving quickly and steadily toward the church. Just before they darted from the last building, three new people showed up at the back door, after everyone else was inside.

"I've seen those guys before. They aren't from around here," Hank said. "Who are they?"

"They're from Little Rock. They're part of the KKK."

"The Ku Klux Klan? That's why the white sheets and hoods. I thought they were all gone from Arkansas. At least, that's what I heard some men in Farmville talking about at church a while back."

"These guys aren't. They aren't ready to give up, yet. They were really happy my dad asked them to come down here."

Hank decided to keep where he'd seen them before to himself for the moment.

"Let's go. Remember, they can't know we're here," Charlie said.

The boys crept to the window where the light shone. Someone opened it and pressed against the screen just as the boys crouched under it. When they heard footsteps move back to the center of the room, Charlie slowly rose to peek in. Hank pulled him down.

"Let me do that," Hank said. "I need to see who's in there. You already know."

"Okay, but be careful. They'll be watching the window and door."

Hank slowly stood to peek from a small corner of the window. There were seven men sitting around a table, in addition to Pinky and his two friends.

"All right, let's get this meeting started," one of the men from Little Rock said. Hank recognized him and the other two from Granny's farm on the morning of the fire.

"Boys, our work is going pretty well. A few more families have left Beech Hill, but we have a lot more to do if we are going to be completely successful."

Charlie stood on the opposite side of the window from Hank and peeked from the lower corner as Hank did.

"Which one is your brother?" Hank said.

"The one guarding the door."

"We could have a problem developing in Farmville, though," the man at the head of the table said.

Hank's interest was piqued.

"The old woman we've been discussing is related to a lawman. Why were we not aware of this before, Pinky?"

"Why are you asking me?" Pinky said. His belligerence cost him a slap across the face from the leader, who backhanded him.

"Watch your mouth, boy. You will speak appropriately to your elders if you want to be part of the Klan. We will not tolerate disrespect or insubordination. Do I make myself clear?"

"Yes, sir," Pinky said. "I'm sorry, sir. It won't happen again. I was unaware of the relationship between the deputy and the old woman till that day. Nothing I had found out from the locals gave any indication that they were family. I knew the deputy was seeing the widow from a neighboring farm, but I was as surprised as you were that he was the old woman's grandson."

"That could have cost us a huge setback. I would suggest you make sure you don't make any more mistakes like that if you wish to remain part of this local chapter."

"Yes, sir. I mean, no, sir. I won't make any more mistakes, sir."

"I'll give you one more chance to prove yourself. I need you to take out that deputy, get him out of the way. Can you do that?"

CHAPTER 10

"Take him out?" Pinky said.

Hank's heart beat so hard and loud in his ears he thought it would give him away.

"Make sure he doesn't keep us from doing what we came here to do. Can you do that, you and your *friends*?"

Hank watched Pinky and his friends nervously look at each other before they all nodded agreement.

"Yeah, we can do it, can't we boys?" Pinky said.

"Good."

"How do you want it done, sir?"

"I don't care how you do it; just make sure we aren't implicated."

"What about the sheriff?" the taller of the other two boys said.

"If he gets in the way, take care of him, too. It'll make my election easier if he's not running against me. Anything else?"

"No, sir," Pinky said.

"Now, we need to talk about the next two missions. I want two raids to happen at the same time. There is a family at Beech Hill who is making a mockery of the fear we are invoking to get the locals to move. That must stop. The other target has a connection to this Beech Hill family. The old woman in Farmville is protecting the boy this family is here with. We need to make sure she stops interfering with our work. It's time to use more persuasive methods. Fire wasn't enough. Fear isn't working. We'll have to use force this time."

"And if someone dies?" Charlie's brother said from the door.

"That isn't the objective, but it wouldn't be the first time," the leader said. "Don't worry, though. The law is on our side. We are doing the work of righteousness. We will be getting rid of a criminal element that cannot be allowed to exist for the town's sake. The sooner we strike the better our chances of succeeding. We need to be ready to go in two nights."

Hank squatted below the window quickly. Charlie joined him.

"What's wrong, Hank?"

"They're talking about Abraham's family and Granny Rose. They're planning on attacking both places at the same time. Charlie, we have to stop them."

"How are we going to do that? There are only two of us."

"I'm not talking about right here, right now. What they're talking about doing is wrong. No matter how they try to put it, they're the ones breaking the law."

"But they're colored people, Hank."

"They're *people*, Charlie. The only difference between them and us is their skin color. Just suppose these men actually do get rid of all the colored people around here. Do you *really* think there won't be anymore trouble?"

"That's what they're saying."

"Think about it. These people won't stop with colored people. Their violence will be turned toward others, maybe their own men in there, who have whatever they want. My daddy always said violence reaps violence. It can't be controlled. Who's to say they won't turn around and start raiding your neighbors, or your own family, who have land they want, next? Your *white* neighbors. Skin color won't be the reason anymore. These men are dangerous. We have to stop them."

"What are you going to do?"

"I don't know, but there's not much time. I've got to get back. I'll let you know tomorrow what we decide to do."

The light from the window went out.

"They're leaving. Don't move," Charlie said.

Both boys pressed close to the outer wall of the church, while the group left from the door just a few feet away.

* * * * * * *

Hank couldn't sleep when he returned to the barn. He hadn't been able to share what he'd learned with Daniel yet.

What am I going to do? If Daddy were here, I'd just go to him. He'd know what to do. Hank turned in his bunk so he could see out the window. *He didn't have to go off to war in France to fight what's right here in our own town. Where are you, God, when stuff like this is happening? Why did my daddy have to die if what he was fighting against doesn't change? Why do good people like Abraham and Granny Rose have to suffer injustice when they're doing what's right? I can't just stand by and let them face this alone. They're my friends. That makes this my fight, too, doesn't it? Abraham has to be wrong. There has to be some kind of change that will let him live his life in peace. I want to do something. I need to help.*

* * * * * * *

Hank awoke with a start. He looked around and saw Daniel and Abraham still asleep in their bunks. It was just getting light outside. A rooster crowed from the chicken yard just beyond the barnyard. *Who let the chickens out?* He tiptoed to the loft window and saw Granny tossing chicken feed to the dozen or so white birds she had raised from little biddies. He returned to his bunk to quickly dress, pausing when both Daniel and Abraham stirred in their sleep. Then he padded down the ladder and across the floor to the barn door. As he approached the chicken yard, he heard Granny humming a hymn while she fed her barnyard animals.

"Morning, Granny."

"Hank, you're up early."

"I could say the same about you. How are you feeling?"

"I'm fine. I really appreciate the work you and your friends have done around here for me, but I'm not used to having someone else do what I've done all my life. I need to get back to my routines."

"I'm glad we could help. I'd ask if I could carry that basket of eggs for you, but I don't want to make you mad or upset you. I just like helping you out." Hank heard the older woman chuckle.

"Here. Be careful not to drop them."

"Thanks, Granny."

They walked to the feed shed and put the bucket back on its nail. Then they walked slowly toward the house.

"You're awful quiet," Granny said. "Something on your mind?"

"Just thinking."

"You miss your daddy, don't you? You wonder why he had to go get himself killed?"

"Partly. How'd you know?" Hank slowed his steps to match Granny's. The love and admiration that filled his heart for her surprised him. *There's more to this lady than she lets on, but it's not what Daniel thinks.*

"I've had to deal with a lot more death and troubles than you have, boy. It's not easy to accept because it wasn't God's plan for any of us to die in the first place. Death was never God's plan. But now that it's a part of our lives, we have to learn how to deal with it and make sense of it."

"Did your daddy die when you were young?"

"Um-hm."

Hank's heart skipped a beat, amazed that they shared something in common. "When did he die."

"When I was a teenager. Someone shot him while we were all doing our chores one morning."

He stopped, overcome with sorrow. "I'm sorry, Granny. I didn't mean to bring up bad memories."

She stopped after taking a couple more steps, turning to face him. "It's okay, Hank. It was a long time ago."

"Did they catch who shot him?"

"No. We were on the reservation, and the government wouldn't let the tribal council look into it. You see, my daddy was a gambler; and he owed a lot of money to several people. I guess one of them made an example out of him to keep others, who owed more, from not paying their debts, too. I left a couple of years later when I got married and never looked back. Those were hard times." She turned and slowly continued toward the house.

Hank thought about his ma, then he realized Granny was almost halfway to the house. He ran to catch up, careful not to spill the eggs from the basket.

"What about your ma?"

"She was already gone. That's why my daddy gambled. He didn't have much to keep him happy after she died."

He thought about Jimmy Jack. "What about your brothers and sisters?"

"I was the youngest. They had all gone their own ways and made new lives for themselves away from the reservation. I was the last to leave."

"Do you ever wonder who did it? Killed your daddy, I mean?"

"No. It's the past. What's done is done. It won't change anything to know who killed him. Everything happens for a reason. I figure I should keep my face toward the future and walk the path God lays out for me, knowing he is there to make everything work out for the best. That's what you're going to have to do, too."

Hank thought about his words carefully before speaking. "I just don't understand why Daddy had to go away when there is so much to fight against right around here. Why did God take him away from me, us, over in France? Maybe he'd still be alive if he'd stayed here."

Granny took the basket from Hank as they reached the yard, forcing him to stop and look at her. "No, Hank. He wouldn't. You see, God knows how long each of us has on this earth. If your daddy had been here, he still would have died when he did. It was his time to go. That's another reason to accept it and move on with your life. You're here for a reason, too. Your daddy fulfilled his reason. He taught you all he was supposed to teach you. Now it's your turn to live the lessons and search for *your* purpose and get about it. Your daddy was a good man. He loved you and your brother and your ma so much he was willing to die for you all."

"But Granny, what did he accomplish dying in France? As far as I can figure it, the same thing he was fighting against over there is what needs to be fought here. So what difference did he make?"

"If you think about it, mankind has been fighting the same fight since time began. Evil doesn't change. As long as there is evil, there will be war of some kind on earth, whether it's halfway across the world or right here in our own backyards. What is accomplished when someone dies is the guarantee there will be someone to take his place."

"What do you mean?"

"Your daddy taught you how to treat people and how to respect life. You are a special young man, Hank. I admire your friendship with Abraham because you don't see his color. You don't see *my* color. You see past the obvious and go straight to the heart of who we are on the inside. Your daddy taught you that. You are keeping those values and beliefs alive and active in your heart. What he can no longer hold, *that truth*, to fight against evil, you are picking up to keep his cause from disappearing. No matter how hard your daddy's death is on you, there is a reason for you to continue where he left off. That's what God has done for you. He has given you a reason to go on."

They went to the pump and washed up before going inside.

"Sometimes I feel so alone, though," he said, splashing water on his face to disguise his tears.

"That's because you're not ready to be alone. You have to search your heart for who God wants to be your teacher and trust him to finish what your daddy started. None of us are meant to be alone. Don't fight against God while you are trying to figure out what he's doing. You're strong, Hank—stronger than most boys your age. You have a powerful character that is being refined as you grow. Don't let your questions keep you from learning. Rather, let your questions guide your journey through the unknown."

"Will you be my teacher, Granny?" Hank saw Granny's face brighten as she smiled.

"Everyone around you is your teacher, as well as anyone you will encounter later in life. God puts people in our lives for a reason. Don't try to find something that may not be there in everything you do. Just let your experiences count for all God would have you be in his time. Now, let's go inside and enjoy the good company God has placed around my table. Go get Daniel and Abraham. Beth Ann should have breakfast just about ready."

"Okay, Granny."

* * * * * * *

As Abraham, Daniel, and Hank worked side by side in the garden at the back of the house later that morning, Hank told his friends what he and Charlie had overheard at the meeting the night before. Before he could tell them who would get visits from the raiders, the boys stopped what they were doing to watch the deputy's sedan and another motor car pull into Granny's yard. Hank watched the three men he had seen at the meeting get out of the second vehicle.

"What are they doing here?" Hank didn't realize he had spoken out loud.

"What?" Abraham said

The boys watched the men shake hands with the deputy before they talked a few minutes where they stood. Hank's heart skipped a beat when he saw concern on the deputy's face. Pete stood with his feet slightly apart and his thumbs hooked along the top of his gun belt. The men shook hands with the deputy again then got back into their vehicle and left.

"I wonder what that was all about," Daniel said.

"Didn't those men help put out the fire the other day, Hank?"

"Yeah. They were at the meeting last night, too."

"What?" Abraham and Daniel said in unison.

CHAPTER 11

"SOMETHING'S NOT RIGHT," HANK SAID. "I'll be right back."

Hank ran to the house, entering through the front door. He heard Deputy Collins and Granny talking on the screened-in back porch.

"They were glad to hear you were doing better, but…" the deputy said.

"Granny. Deputy Collins," Hank said from the kitchen.

"Out here, Hank. What's wrong, son?"

He felt a surprising jolt of comfort at the familiar tag Deputy Collins used just then. He heard genuine concern in his voice, too. There was a scowl on the deputy's face, and his eyebrows came together in a furrow.

"Is everything all right?" Hank said. "I saw those men with you out there."

"It's nothing you need to worry about. I need you, Daniel, and Abraham to stay close to the house today, though. I don't want Beth Ann and Granny to be left alone, you hear?"

"Sure. Is Ma okay?"

"Yeah. I'm bringing her and Jimmy Jack over here later this afternoon. She's going to help Granny do some canning. Don't alarm them, though, when you see them. I have to look into something tonight. It could be nothing, but I need to check it out anyway."

"How about some coffee, Deputy?" Beth Ann said. She carefully cradled a cup of steaming coffee in both hands.

"Thanks but I have to go right now. Later, okay?"

The deputy gave Granny a kiss on the cheek and ruffled Hank's hair as he left through the house. Hank followed him to the front parlor.

"See you later, Mr. Pete."

Beth Ann joined Hank in the front parlor, both watching through the screen as the deputy left in a hurry.

"I need to tell you what I heard him tell Granny," she said.

"Let's take this outside. I don't want Granny to hear. Come on. Daniel and Abraham are out back. We can talk there."

Daniel and Abraham were just leaving the garden when they approached.

"Everything all right?" Daniel said.

"No," Beth Ann said. "There's trouble coming, according to what Deputy Collins was telling Granny."

"Maybe we'd better wait till we're in the barn to discuss this," Hank said.

The four friends carried the gardening tools to the barn. Once they were inside, Abraham made sure all was secure.

"What's going on?" Daniel said.

"Those men who drove up at the same time as Deputy Collins told him they had overheard talk in Snow Hill," Beth Ann said. "He said something about a riot that was brewing at Beech Hill tonight. Someone said something about a possible lynching, too. He's going to get Sheriff Stan, so they can try to head it off."

"What are they trying to do?" Hank said.

"What do you mean?" Daniel said. "Who are you talking about?"

"I need to warn the deputy. Those men are part of the Klan. They're planning a raid out there for *tomorrow* night. Something doesn't feel right about this. He's bringing Ma and Jimmy Jack out here later. I need to tell him what I know when he gets here. If I don't see him first, don't let him leave without talking with me, okay, Beth Ann?"

"Wait. I'm confused," Daniel said. "I thought you said those men were at the meeting last night, so why are they here today like they're on our side?"

"Exactly what I'm talking about. The guy who talked with Deputy Collins just now was part of the meeting last night. The shorter guy was the one in charge."

"You said they were planning two attacks. Did they say where they would be going?" Abraham said.

"Yeah. Beech Hill and here."

"Here?" Daniel and Beth Ann said in unison.

"Is my family in danger?"

"I think so, Abraham."

"I've got to go to them. Tell Granny I'll be back as soon as I'm able."

"Wait, Abraham," Hank said.

Abraham ran out the barn door and into the woods that led to Beech Hill.

"What's the plan?" Beth Ann said.

"It's happening too fast. I'm not sure what to do."

"I say we let the sheriff and the deputy handle this, Hank," Daniel said. "What can we do if they have guns?"

"Let's cross that bridge when we come to it, okay?" Hank said. "We need to get to the house. Granny's alone and shouldn't be. We'll all stay close to her till the deputy gets back."

"What do we tell her about Abraham?" Beth Ann said.

"The truth. I need to tell her what I know about tomorrow night. This has gone way beyond the four of us, now."

As they were walking toward the house, Hank saw a tall blond-haired boy run out of the woods from the direction of Snow Hill.

"Daniel, look. It's Charlie."

The three friends watched Charlie fall. They all ran; but Hank got to him first.

"Charlie, are you okay?"

Charlie was lying face down on the ground. Hank was about to turn him over when Beth Ann reached them.

"Don't turn him over, yet. We need to check for injuries, first."

Hank stepped back, watching Beth Ann examine him, just like her father does with patients. Daniel joined them, out of breath.

"No broken bones that I can tell. Let's turn him over. But be careful."

They all three carefully turned him over. His face was puffy and pale. His nose was bleeding, and there was a cut on both of his cheeks.

"What happened to him?" Beth Ann said.

"Pinky," Hank and Daniel said at the same time.

* * * * * * *

"How's he doing," Granny said.

"Still sleeping," Beth Ann said.

"Young lady, you are going to make a fine doctor."

"Thanks, Granny."

Hank and Daniel stayed with Charlie while he slept. They had watched Granny treat his cuts and bruises with Beth Ann at her side. Hank was impressed that Daniel had set aside his fear of Granny while she tended their new friend. Charlie woke up briefly while she was sewing the deeper cut on his left cheek, but he slept now from the herbal concoction Beth Ann had put in some tea for him. It must have tasted awful from the face he made.

"When's he going to wake up?" Daniel said. "He must have something important to tell us if he came all the way here."

"Sleep is good for him, but he should be awake before long," Granny said.

Charlie moaned, slowly moving his head from side to side. His actions reminded Hank of his brother when Jimmy Jack was waking from a bad dream.

"Daniel, you and Hank stay close so you are the first faces he sees," Granny said.

The boys sat on either side of him on the bed. Granny and Beth Ann left the room.

"Hank…you've got to…warn them."

"Who, Charlie?"

"Abraham's family…and Granny. They're going…tonight. The raids…are tonight…instead of…tomorrow night."

"Charlie, who did this to you?" Daniel said.

"Pinky…and his…friends. I didn't…have his money. When my…brother stopped them…Pinky told him…I knew about… the raids. He got…so mad. He told…Pinky to plan…to ride… tonight. He…left to tell…the others…and I came here."

"Daniel, I've got to warn Abraham."

"What do you want me to do?"

"Stay here. Make sure Deputy Collins knows what's going on when he gets back. I can't wait. I need to go now. Tell Granny what Charlie told us and help her and Beth Ann get ready. Go to the storm cellar, if nothing else, to stay safe."

"Okay, Hank. Be careful."

* * * * * * *

When Hank arrived at Beech Hill, all appeared peaceful. A scream broke the serenity of the mid-afternoon quiet. Hank ran in the direction of the woman's cries.

"You leave my boy alone. He didn't do anything to you."

He found the tent where the commotion was coming from and entered.

"Abraham," he said.

"Well, well, well. Look who we've got here," Pinky said. He pointed a double-barreled shotgun at Hank from the back of Abraham's ma's tent. He heard muffled grunts and saw a couple of others beating on someone in the far corner. Hank made an attempt to go to Abraham.

"Don't be stupid. They won't kill him, but they will make him wish he'd never come here and brought his family with him."

"Why? What did he do to you?" Hank wanted to do something, but his body wouldn't move.

"Are you blind? Don't you see what these people are doing to our community? They're taking over the land, keeping wages down, and robbing honest folks of earning a decent living. If we don't stop it now, we won't have anything left."

"That's crazy, Pinky, and you know it. There's enough land and money to go around. People who have made themselves judges of the very things they are blinded to in their own lives are poisoning you. Think about it. The fear you're talking about didn't exist before they came here. Why do you think they have *you* doing their dirty work?"

"Shut up. You don't know what you're talking about. You're part of the problem. If it weren't for people like you, these people would know their place and stay where they belong. As far as I'm concerned, you're just like them."

Hank turned tearful eyes toward Abraham's ma.

"I'm so sorry."

"That's enough, guys," Pinky said. "Let's go. We've done our duty here."

Each of the boys kicked Abraham one more time before following Pinky out of the tent. Hank ran to Abraham's unconscious body. His ma was on the other side of him, cradling Abraham's limp body, rocking him back and forth in her arms as if he were a baby. Tears streamed down her face.

"I'll be back with help, ma'am."

Hank ran all the way to Farmville. He burst through Dr. Warden's office and crumbled from exhaustion just inside the door.

CHAPTER 12

"**H**ANK, WHAT'S WRONG? IS BETH Ann all right?"

"She's fine, Dr. Warden. It's Abraham." Hank was so out of breath, he spoke in a hoarse whisper. "You've got to go to him. He's at Beech Hill. He's been beaten really badly. I don't know if he's dead or alive."

"Come on, son. Let's get you some water. Then you can take me to Abraham."

The drive to Beech Hill took far less time than the run through the woods, but it felt like forever to Hank. A crowd had gathered around the tent where Abraham's family lived.

"He's in there, Doc. Please help him."

Dr. Warden gently pushed his way through the crowd. Hank stayed close behind him.

"Please let me through. Let me get to my patient, please."

The tent was full of people from the Beech Hill community.

"I need you all to go outside so I can see to Abraham, folks. Please, clear the room except for his mother."

Abraham's ma grabbed Hank by the upper arm in a vise-like grip.

"Thank you, young man. You're a *good* friend to my boy. Thank you for bringing the doctor, but what about *your* family?"

"They're safe. Please don't make me leave, yet."

"Suit yourself. Would you please run down to the river and get some water for the doctor?"

"Yes, ma'am." Hank grabbed the bucket just inside the tent and ran to the river.

It won't be long before it's dark. Then what?

When Hank got back to the tent, Sheriff Stan and Deputy Collins were there.

"Hank, son, what are you doing here?"

"Deputy Collins, I came to warn Abraham and his family; but I was too late. Pinky and his friends did this. I think there may be more trouble out here when it gets dark."

"I know, Daniel told me. We'll talk later about your going back to Snow Hill without permission. Right now, we need to get you back to Granny Rose's and out of harm's way here."

"No, I want to stay."

"Hank, I don't have time to argue with you about this. This is a legal matter. Your mother is very worried about you, son. You need to go."

"Please. I need to stay with Abraham."

"Pete, these people are getting ugly out here. I need you to stay here while I go back to Granny Rose's. I know she's family, but you'll be more help here than there."

"Will you take Hank back with you?"

"Sure. Come on, son."

"I'm sorry, Sheriff. I won't go. Please, Mr. Pete, I can't go. I need to stay with my friend. If you make me go, sir, I'll just run back here as soon as I can."

"Hank…"

"It might be a good idea for him to stay, especially if Abraham wakes up," Doc said. "It might be good to see a friendly face."

The deputy thoughtfully looked from the sheriff to the doctor to Hank. He nodded.

"Thanks, Stan. From what I've been told, there's definitely trouble headed to Granny's tonight."

"Don't you worry about her or anyone else there. I'll get several of the men from town over there to keep it from getting out of hand. We'll put them in the storm cellar till it's all clear."

"Sounds good. I'll get these people organized and ready for what's coming here. I'd rather be with my family, though, if you want to know the truth."

"I know, but what they say about doctors treating their own kin, and lawyers defending their own family, is true for this situation, too. Take care, now. Don't worry about your family. They'll be in good hands. It's going to be a long night, though."

"God speed, Stan."

"We'll be praying for you all out here."

"We're going to need it."

* * * * * * *

Hank stood near the front of the tent while Doc tended Abraham's wounds. The light inside the tent was growing dim as the afternoon sun slowly slipped low on the horizon. *I failed him, Daddy. I thought I could handle this myself, but I've failed. I almost got my friend killed today. I'm scared for Mr. Pete and Sheriff Stan. This is more than I can do by myself. No matter how much I want to be the man you were, I'm not. What am I going to do? I need to warn the deputy and sheriff about Pinky, but will I only be putting them in more danger by telling them? I don't know what to do!*

"Hank?" the deputy said. "We need to talk, son; but not in here."

Hank hadn't realized the deputy had come inside or spoken with Doc.

"How's he doing?"

"He'll be just fine," the deputy said. "Doc said he has some broken ribs, so I guess you and Daniel are going to have to take care of Granny's chores while he heals."

Hank nodded, but his sad smile didn't quite reach his eyes.

"Come on, son. Let's go outside to talk."

They quietly walked to the river.

"Let's sit over on these rocks, Hank."

The last rays of sunlight gave way to dusk as they sat. The deputy had picked up a few pebbles and skipped a couple of them across the river's surface before saying anything.

"Daniel told me what you learned while at Snow Hill last night. What I need to know is why you thought you couldn't tell me and let me handle it?"

"I…I'm sorry. I really didn't think…"

The deputy's anger exploded.

"That's right. You didn't think." Hank couldn't tell if he was just angry or scared or both. "Do you know what kind of danger you put yourself in by eavesdropping on that meeting? What's it going to take for you to realize you can trust me, Hank? When I heard what you had done, my heart stopped. All I could think about was all of the 'what ifs' that could make the scene in that tent up the hill over there a reality for you, your ma, and your brother. How do you think I would have felt, knowing I couldn't protect you from that because you wanted to handle it yourself? Did you stop to think the sheriff and I might have already been watching this group?" The deputy took a deep breath and slowly released it. When he spoke again, there was a different kind of concern in his voice that Hank recognized from Sunday evening. "I know you feel you have something to prove with your dad gone and all; but you are just a boy, Hank. Leave this to the professionals." The deputy threw a couple more pebbles out across the river. Hank heard them splash.

"Does Ma know?" Hank leaned back on his hands, his elbows trembling.

"No. I didn't want to frighten her; but she isn't blind, Hank. You don't give her any more credit than you do me for what we *do* know. Look, I admire you and your friends for how they have pitched in to help. You, Daniel, Beth Ann, and Abraham stick together like family. You each have talents that bring you together in a way that works well when the time is right. I know you want to be helpful and use those talents for good. If you'd give me the chance, I could help you all learn how to use them without putting you in the danger *you've* put *yourself* into."

"I thought I was doing the right thing protecting all of you. I really didn't think Pinky's threats would put anyone in danger if I kept them to myself."

The deputy put his arm around Hank's shoulders.

"I know." His voice was calmer, gentle. "You probably didn't think there was anything to the threats, either. I remember what it was like when I was your age. I used to get into so much trouble because my solution was to fight my way through everything. What I learned was that I was only fighting myself, not the problems. Once I realized that, I was able to see where my strength really came from—the people around me and all they could teach me. It's important to accept your limitations and trust those around you to lend a hand. Learn to grow through your weaknesses and become strong from the lessons learned, rather than taking the easy road around the problems. You'll learn it's okay to be weak or not know what to do as long as you are willing to set aside the fear of the unknown to make that weakness your strength."

"You sound so much like my daddy, Mr. Pete. That scares me sometimes."

"It's okay. I understand, really. I've told you before, and I still mean it. I'm not trying to take your father's place in your life. Granny would say my being a part of your life is like an extension of your father."

"She was telling me something like that earlier this morning. She said there would be someone to take up where he left off, so I would be able to carry on what he started."

"That's right. It's an honor to be here for you, Hank. Your father was a special man. I don't think I could ever be like him; but I've found myself caring for you, and your ma and brother, more than I thought I ever could care for anyone. In a way, *that* scares *me*." Hank felt the chill of the early evening on his shoulders when Deputy Collins removed his arm from around them. "Before I came here, I prided myself on not needing to have anyone but me to take care of. Now? What if I fail? What if I don't live up to your expectations, or your ma's or Jimmy Jack's?"

Hank thought about the fears that hounded him lately. "How do I stop being afraid?"

"What are you afraid of?"

"I'm afraid I'll forget my daddy. I'm afraid if I love someone else like I do him I'll lose that person, too."

"You'll never forget your father, Hank. You can't. Every time you look in the mirror, you'll see him. When you hear Jimmy Jack's voice, you'll hear him. He'll always be there because he's part of you and your brother. No one can take that away from you. You'll have to work through your fears yourself. No one can do that for you, but don't let it rob you of the happiness your father would want you to have. He died so you can enjoy the life he wanted for you."

"Do you think he would want someone, like you, to take his place?"

"I can't speak for him, but *I'd* want you to have someone to be there for you if *I* couldn't be there to finish what I had started."

"How will I know who the right person is to take over his place in our family?"

"By trusting your heart with what it is telling you about those who come into your life."

"But what if I'm wrong? What if I'm too late? What if I…"

A shot rang out from the trees behind them in the late light of dusk. Deputy Collins fell to the ground in a heap, unconscious.

"Deputy Collins? Mr. Pete?"

Hank jumped from the rock. He struggled to roll the deputy onto his side and saw several dark splotches on the sand. He felt something sticky on his hand. Then he saw blood spread as it soaked the back of the deputy's shirt just under his collarbone and to the left of his right shoulder blade. Panic and fear paralyzed Hank's ability to think momentarily.

"Somebody, help."

CHAPTER 13

Hank shook the deputy's uninjured shoulder. "Wake up. Please, wake up." His heart ached as fear forced the blood through his veins. Tears flowed freely down his face.

"Don't you die on me." Panic threatened to take his ability to think. "Please, somebody, help."

Thankfully, he remembered Dr. Warden was still with Abraham. He gently rolled the injured deputy onto his back and ran for help. Darkness closed in fast. Lanterns inside the tents illuminated the community and guided Hank's way to where Dr. Warden would be. Several men from Beech Hill had gathered along the trail leading to the river. Each had a rifle or shotgun.

"Boy, are you hurt? We heard a gunshot."

Hank recognized the man who spoke from the day before. He had been the one guiding the logging team.

"It's Deputy Collins. He's been shot. I've got to get Doc Warden."

Hank ignored the voices as he ran past the men. As he approached Abraham's ma's tent, he saw Dr. Warden come around the corner.

"Doc," he said. "Doc, you've got to come quick."

"Hank, what's wrong? Where's Pete?"

Hank nearly collapsed into the doctor's arms.

"Doc, Mr. Pete's been shot. He's down at the river."

"Let me get my bag, son. Catch your breath. I'll be right back."

He was only gone a few seconds, but it seemed like hours for Hank. Everything moved in very slow motion.

"Show me," Dr. Warden said.

They ran along the trail to the river. It felt as though his feet were made of lead. Hank noticed that the men who had been on the trail just a few minutes earlier were gone. *Where'd they go?* Hank stopped several feet from the deputy. He saw a couple of the Beech Hill men kneeling next to him. It looked as if they were protecting the deputy from unseen predators, the way they kept watching the tree lines on both sides of the river.

"He's over there, Doc," Hank said, unable to move forward out of fear. All he could do was point and stare in the direction of the two men standing guard.

"Oh, dear Lord," Doc said. "You stay back while I check him out, son."

The men watching over the deputy stood as the doctor ran the last few feet to the fallen lawman. One of them was the large, muscular logger man from Snow Hill. Hank couldn't see exactly what Doc was doing, but there was urgency in his movements. Hank slowly stepped forward and stood just behind the doctor, frozen in place. *God, please don't let him die, too.*

"Men, help me get him back up the hill. I need to get that bullet out. I'll need a table."

"We'll take him to my tent, doctor. It's closer," the logger man said. "You can tend to him there. Whatever you need, let me know."

"Good. Thank you, sir." Dr. Warden said, shaking the big man's hand before the two colored men carefully lifted the deputy.

"How bad is it, Doc?" Hank said as he and the doctor stepped out of the way of the path.

"I won't know till I get him in the light," he said. He put his arm around Hank's shoulders. "Now, don't jump to conclusions, son, before I get the chance to look him over properly. He's a strong man. It's not just a flesh wound; but I don't think it's a life-threatening wound, either. With the proper care, he should be just fine in a couple of weeks. It's a good thing whoever shot him wasn't so good with his aim. It could've been a lot worse."

* * * * * * *

Hank sat on the ground at the foot of a large sweet gum tree outside the tent where Dr. Warden operated on Deputy Collins. His stomach was so tied up in knots he felt as if he would throw up.

"I should've told him about Pinky's threat, Daddy. Maybe if I had he wouldn't have been shot. He would have been watching his back instead of having to scold me. I've messed up so badly. What's Ma going to do? She's finally happy for the first time in years, and I've ruined it for her. I never thought any of this would happen. How do I fix it?"

Hank folded his arms across his knees and lowered his head onto them. His shoulders shuddered as the tears that flooded his soul overflowed from his eyes.

"Hank?" Hank jerked his head up at the doctor's call from the tent. His nerves pricked his skin in anxious anticipation. He squinted his eyes against the bright light that shone through the doorway. The doctor stood just outside the shelter, wiping his hands with a light-colored towel. His shirtsleeves were still rolled up around his elbows. Hank slowly stood, afraid to walk toward him.

"Hank? Where are you, son?"

"I'm here, sir. Is he going to be all right?" Dr. Warden joined Hank under the tree.

"He'll be sore for a few days, but he should heal nicely. The bullet is out, and he's sleeping. I need you to sit with him. Would you mind? Let me know if a fever develops? Infection is always a danger with nonfatal gunshot wounds. I want to check in on Abraham."

"What about the sheriff? Shouldn't he be told the deputy's been shot?"

"Someone's already gone to Granny Rose's to tell him."

"What do you think he'll do?" Hank said.

"I don't know, but these people need to know that they have friends around here. I'm not going anywhere till I know Abraham and Pete are out of danger. You know, it's a shame more *men* aren't like you, Hank Baker. You're a fine example for all of us, me included."

Hank took a shaky, deep breath. "It's what my daddy would have done."

"I know, son. I know. With your courage, maybe more will follow your lead."

"I don't know if that's such a good idea, though. I've messed things up so much. If I had only told him earlier…"

"Look, son. You couldn't have known this was going to happen. You can't blame yourself for someone else's choices."

"What about *my* choices?" Hank said. He angrily wiped at the tears that flooded his eyes again. The doctor took Hank gently by both shoulders and got down on his level, eye to eye.

"Learn from your mistakes and make better choices the next time. Come on, now. I need to see about Abraham. Go to your Mr. Pete," Dr. Warden said. His smile and encouraging squeeze gave Hank some comfort. "It'll be a while before he wakes up, but it'll be good for him to see a familiar face. I don't want him trying to get up too soon and make those stitches bleed. Have someone come get me when he wakes up, will you?"

"Okay, Doc, be careful. I don't think we've seen the last of the trouble around here tonight."

"You be careful, too."

* * * * * * *

Hank timidly stepped into the tent, pausing near the entrance. He avoided looking at the man who lay on the table in the middle of the room as long as he could. There was a pot-bellied stove in the far, left corner, an icebox in the other corner. A rocking chair was just to the right of the entrance and a single bed lined the wall on the left. When there was nothing else to look at, Hank stared as the deputy breathed in what appeared to be peaceful sleep. He was still lying on his stomach. The bandage wrapped around his right shoulder had a large spot of blood staining it where the bullet had been removed. Hank quietly sat in the rocking chair. He kept his eyes on the deputy's slowly breathing form.

Only a coward shoots a man in the back. Only a coward lets someone else do his dirty work, but this isn't Pinky's style. Who could have done this? As he replayed the event in his mind, Hank began to cry, again. Then he angrily wiped his eyes dry. *I was sitting right next to him. It should have been* me *that was shot*—not Mr. Pete. *He's a good man. I'm* the one who keeps messing up. He knows what to do when the Klan gets here. I *don't.* He raised angry eyes toward heaven.

"Why did you let this happen, God? What have I *done* to make you so mad? When are you going to stop using the ones I care about to *punish* me? First it was Daddy, then Charlie and Abraham, now Mr. Pete."

Before Hank had time to consider that last startling revelation, the deputy stirred slightly and moaned. His brooding thoughts vanished. He stood, watching cautiously. When all was still and quiet again, he slowly stepped up to the table. He flexed his fists at his sides before reaching to straighten the sheet over the deputy. Heat radiated from the sleeping man's exposed flesh. Hank fetched the washbasin from the top of the icebox. After wringing out the cool water, he carefully bathed the deputy's face. He had watched his ma do the same when Jimmy Jack had chicken pox last month. He set the cloth back in the cool water and pulled up a ladder back chair. The deputy's breathing became slow and steady again. Then, and only then, did the nerves in Hank's stomach and knees calm.

"I'm so sorry, Mr. Pete," he said. "I wish it had been me that had gotten shot instead of you. These people need you, not me, when the Klan gets here later tonight. I don't know what to do to stop them." He reached up and gently laid a hand on the deputy's uninjured shoulder.

"Granny was right, you know. She said there would be someone in my life who would take over where my daddy left off. You're right, too. I have to listen to my heart and trust it to tell me who that person is," Hank said. He hesitated a moment. His heart painfully pounded against his chest. "I don't know if you can hear me, but I need to tell you something." He moved the chair closer to the table. "The more I fight it, the more convinced I am of what I already know in my heart. *You're* that person, Mr. Pete. You said you were honored to be part of my life, but I don't deserve that honor. I've been nothing but trouble to you since you came along. I'm so sorry…really. When I think about it, *I'm* the one who's honored that *you're* here for *me*." Hank sat back and clasped his hands tightly in his lap to keep them from shaking. "My daddy would've chosen you to take his place if he had known you. I know he would've. You're so much like him; but you're different, too. I have a lot to learn. Will you teach me? Will you take over where my father left off?"

Hank became silent when he heard someone enter the tent; but he didn't move, thinking it was one of the men.

"Hey, how's everything out here? Wow, what happened to him?"

Hank started at the familiar voice, somewhat relieved until he thought about the possible meaning behind his friend's presence.

"Daniel, why aren't you at Granny's?" he said. He could feel the blood drain from his face. "Is something wrong?"

"Probably, Pinky's looking for you."

CHAPTER 14

Daniel tiptoed into the light and joined Hank at the table. His eyes grew wide with recognition.

"That's Deputy Collins. What happened? Is he going to be all right?"

"What are you doing here? You're supposed to be with Beth Ann, Granny, Ma, and Jimmy Jack. Why'd you come here?"

"I came with Charlie. He wanted to be here when his brother came."

"Who's with the others?"

"The sheriff got a bunch of the men from town to come out to Granny's. You ought to see it. It's like they're getting ready for an Indian attack. You know, like the ones described in those old dime novels. They've set a trap for anyone who dares to set foot on her property and try anything. You don't have anything to worry about over there, believe me. How did *this* happen?"

"We were down at the river talking when someone shot him in the back right after sundown," Hank said, his face burned and tingled as the blood returned. "You said Pinky was looking for me? When did you see him last? I need to know if he had anything to do with this."

"Why would Pinky do this?"

"He was ordered to take the deputy out. Remember what I told you about the meeting? Now, when did you see him last?"

"It couldn't have been Pinky. He was at Granny's till sundown. I saw him and two others just before I heard them ride off on horses. Don't worry, though. The sheriff has the men watching in shifts all night long, to keep them all safe over there."

"Does he know you and Charlie are here?" Hank said.

"I wanted to tell him, but Charlie was afraid he'd try to stop him. I tell you, though, I think that man has eyes in the back of his head. Just when you think you've given him the slip, he shows up when you least expect it. So he *might* know. What I *do* know is that Charlie said he wanted to try to talk some sense into his brother before something terrible happens. I didn't want him to come alone, in case his brother wouldn't listen. I heard your voice when I went looking for you and Abraham, and followed it. So here I am."

"Did you see anything along the way here?"

"Not from the Klan, but we did see a couple of colored men with shotguns running in the direction of Granny's farm. Who do you suppose they were?"

"Doc said someone had gone to tell the sheriff about Mr. Pete's getting shot. I guess that could have been them."

"Did you warn Abraham in time?"

"No," Hank said, sighing with defeat. "Daniel, I've made such a mess of things by keeping Pinky's threats a secret. When I got here, two guys were beating him up pretty badly. They were with Pinky. Doc says he's got some broken ribs."

"Oh, man."

"He's going to need to heal before he's able to work around Granny's farm much. I told Doc we'd be able to help out as long as we're needed."

Daniel swallowed hard.

"H-how long will that be? W-will we have to stay with Granny while he's getting well?"

Hank couldn't help grinning. It felt good to let go of some of his fear and anxiety, even for a brief moment. "What if we did? It wouldn't be so bad, now, would it?"

Daniel vigorously nodded his head several times. "Yes, it would."

"Look, I'll make you a deal," Hank said, giggling softly. "If we get out of this alive and someone needs to stay with Granny Rose while Abraham gets well, I'll stay. You can go home every night. Just don't be late the next morning."

"Deal. Wait, what happens if I'm late?"

The deputy tried to turn over and moaned, startling both boys. Hank went to him, feeling his forehead like Ma did when he or Jimmy Jack was sick.

"He's waking up. Go get Doc, will you? And tell him his skin is really hot."

Daniel quickly backed out of the tent, then turned and ran. Hank retrieved the washbasin to bathe the deputy's hot face, hoping it would keep him from stirring too much. It took mere seconds for the cool cloth to feel hotter from the fever than before. He soaked the cloth with cool water a couple of times before the deputy stopped trying to turn over.

"It's okay, Mr. Pete. Calm down. Please, don't move. You'll start bleeding again. Daniel's gone to get Doc. Just hold on."

Hank's heart pounded against his chest with each aching beat. Sweat stung his eyes as he hurriedly tended the sleeping man.

"Hank, I'm here, son," Dr. Warden said as he entered the tent.

He stepped back from the deputy to let the doctor take over.

"You've done a good job here. Why don't you go to Daniel outside?"

Neither of the boys spoke for a long time, waiting under the sweet gum tree for word. Hank kept the doctor in his line of sight from outside as he tended to the deputy. After several minutes, Daniel placed a friendly hand on his shoulder.

"What do you want to do now," Daniel said.

"I don't know. I can't seem to do anything right lately. You want to know the truth?"

"What?"

"I'm scared. I can't stop the Klan when they get here, not like Mr. Pete would have. We're all alone with the sheriff at Granny's and Mr. Pete in there on that table unconscious."

"I didn't think about that."

"I'm so sorry I got you into this, Daniel."

"Hey, you didn't make me do anything I didn't want to do. Well, except maybe stay at Granny's, but…"

"What if someone gets killed here tonight? It'll be my fault because I just *had* to do this myself." Panic put a tremor in Hank's voice. "I could have told the sheriff about Pinky and his 'night' friends, but I didn't. I'm to blame for Abraham getting beat up, for Mr. Pete getting shot, and for whatever else happens here and at Granny Rose's later tonight."

"No, you aren't."

"*Yes, I am,*" Hank said. He squared off in front of Daniel and grabbed both his shoulders. "You need to go; leave here. Don't let me get you hurt, too."

"I'm not leaving."

Hank dropped his hands to his sides and stared at Daniel in disbelief. Then he turned his back on his best friend for the first time in his life.

"Go, Daniel, *go home*. I don't *need* you here. I don't *want* you here."

Daniel placed a hand on Hank's shoulder.

"But, Hank, you're my friend. I'm not leaving without you."

Hank shook off Daniel's hand before facing him again.

"If you stay, you won't be my friend anymore."

Daniel stepped away from Hank, shaking his head. Hank noticed the set to Daniel's jaw and the flash of anger in his eyes.

"*I'm not leaving.*"

"Suit yourself, then. Get hurt or killed, for all I care, if that's what you want. Just stay out of my way."

"What are you going to do?"

"That's none of your business. You don't have to worry about me anymore; but I'm telling you, if you stay, our friendship is officially over."

Daniel's expression softened.

"Hank, you're not making sense."

Hank stepped forward and pushed Daniel to the ground.

"Don't you get it? I don't *care* anymore. I *can't* care. Everyone I care about winds up hurt or dead. If you know what's good for you, you'll get as far away from me as possible."

Hank turned and ran hard for the river. Tears stung his eyes as the branches slapped his face and scratched his arms. He was in unfamiliar territory. When he reached the river, he fell to his knees at the water's edge and sobbed. A twig snapped behind him. He stopped crying, but didn't move, listening intently to the sound of someone walking up behind him. Anger replaced pain.

"Daniel, *leave me alone.*"

"I'm not your little buddy, Hank Baker."

Hank slowly stood without turning around to face Pinky. His fingers felt numb from his tightly clenched fists, shaking at his sides.

"I understand you're looking for me. What do you want?" Hank said.

"I wanted to see for myself how the high and mighty Hank Baker was holding up. You've been busy. I'm impressed. How does it feel to be a hero?"

Hank turned and shoved Pinky to the ground. Before the bully had the chance to react, Hank sat on him and grabbed two fistfuls of the older boy's shirt. He lifted Pinky's shoulders off the ground; their faces were only a couple of inches apart. Hank's eyes flashed barely controlled red, hot anger.

"Why'd you do it?"

"I don't know what you're talking about." Hank could almost smell the fear coming from Pinky's shaking body.

"Why'd you shoot the deputy?"

"Shoot the...what? I didn't shoot anybody, I swear. I just got here."

Hank ignored the fear that was obvious in the other boy's voice.

"You know who did. *Tell me.*"

"I don't know anything about what you're saying."

Hank finally heard the terror in Pinky's answers. He released his grip and stepped away from the fight that had almost taken over Hank's senses.

"Why are you here? I thought you were supposed to be 'taking care' of Granny while your *'night'* friends did their business here," Hank said.

Pinky stood and slapped the sand off his shoulders, backside, and trousers legs.

"Believe it or not, I came to help you. I couldn't come till I knew Granny would be safe. The sheriff was supposed to be right behind me. I guess he was delayed."

"Why would you want to help me?" Hank said. His suspicions clouded his words, and his cheeks grew hot. His fists tightened at his sides, again.

"Look, those guys you saw me with in Snow Hill and I got into some trouble a while back in Smackover," Pinky said. "That mayor, Clyde Byrd, gave us a choice. Go to jail or work off our time helping a friend with a little problem. That friend was

Sheriff Stan. We didn't want to go to jail, so we agreed to his offer."

Pinky sat on his haunches and rested his forearms across his knees as he clasped his hands under his chin.

"We've been working with Sheriff Stan and your Deputy Collins for a couple of weeks, now. I guess they're trying to keep another incident like Cross Roads from happening. There's a group of men who've been causing trouble with the colored people here at Beech Hill. The sheriff was pretty sure it was based in Snow Hill, but he wasn't positive. Since *we're* from Snow Hill, he and that mayor thought we could keep our eyes and ears open to find out who was involved and turn them in."

"How do I know you're telling the truth?"

"You don't, I guess," Pinky said, his tone somewhere between sarcasm and defeat.

Hank couldn't see the older boy's face, so he listened carefully to his voice for clues in the moonless, cloudy night. Pinky sighed.

"I'm sorry about the deputy; but I really didn't have anything to do with his getting shot."

Hank didn't move, and his fists remained clenched.

"Listen, I heard what you said to Daniel back there. This isn't your fault."

Hank relaxed a little and sat next to Pinky on the sand.

"What about that fight in the churchyard? Are you saying that was just for show?"

"Yeah, pretty good, huh? You were pretty good yourself."

Hank wasn't sure what to think about Pinky's response. He seemed to have a respectful tone in his voice.

"I had to do something because Charlie's brother caught me spying on one of their meetings," Pinky said. "It was the first one the Little Rock men headed up. I had to make them think I wanted to help 'cleanse' Beech Hill. That fight, among other things, was my proof to them that I was as bad as I said I was. I was being watched and my loyalties were being tested. That's why I was so loud. If I had failed Sheriff Stan, I know he would have sent me back to Mayor Byrd. And I would have ended up in jail."

"Well, what about the fight with Charlie today? Was that for show, too?"

"What are you talking about?"

"Oh, come on, Pinky. He showed up at Granny's all beat up. He said you had your boys do it because you didn't get your money."

"I swear, Hank. I didn't have anything to do with that, either. But Charlie *is* the reason I was looking for you. When I saw you and Daniel with him in Snow Hill, I almost passed out. Be very careful, Hank. Charlie and his brother make *me* look like a nice guy, even when I'm not."

"What are you saying?"

"I'm…"

An explosion of glowing, yellow firelight suddenly lit up the area just over the hill from the river. Gunfire shattered the peacefulness of the night.

"It's begun," Pinky said. "Come on, Hank. We really are on the same side here. I'll explain anything you want later. Partners?"

Hank reluctantly shook Pinky's offered hand before standing up.

"Let's go. We need to do what we can till the sheriff gets here," Pinky said.

CHAPTER 15

As Hank and Pinky topped the hill, people were running in every direction. Lamps inside tents were extinguished.

"Wait," Hank said. "What's the plan? We need a plan."

Several horses with white-hooded riders made a curved line that stretched the length of the compound. The large burning cross had been erected in front of one tent in particular.

"That's Abraham's ma's tent," Hank said, his heart racing.

"What do you want to do?" Pinky said.

Hank watched someone running through the compound in their direction.

"Hank," Daniel said.

He was out of breath when he reached the two boys at the top of the hill.

"Pinky?"

Hank glanced at the Snow Hill bully and decided he had to give him the benefit of the doubt.

"He's here to help, Daniel. Where's Doc?"

"He's still with Deputy Collins."

"Where's Charlie?" Pinky said.

"Why?"

"Where is he, Daniel?" Hank said.

"I'm not sure where he went. I haven't seen him since we got here."

"Well, he's either on one of those horses; or he's searching the tents for the deputy," Pinky said. "Most likely, they know he isn't dead; and they'll want to make an example out of him for anyone who tries to stop them. If I had to guess, I'd say Charlie's brother is the one who shot him. Once they knew the law was here, they would have had someone make sure he didn't interfere. Since I was at Granny's, I'm pretty sure Floyd Hutch would have volunteered to do it."

"What's he saying, Hank? Charlie isn't one of them. You heard him yesterday."

"I think we've got to trust Pinky on this one. He's been a lot closer to Charlie than we have. I'll explain everything later. Right now, we need to make sure they don't find the deputy and Doc. We need to get them to safety. I sure hope someone got Abraham and his family out of that tent before any of this started."

"I'll look for Charlie," Pinky said. "You two take care of the deputy and the doctor. If I don't know where you've taken them, I can't tell them anything."

"All right. Let's go, Daniel. Pinky, be careful. These guys are dangerous."

"I know."

Pinky ran toward the tree line.

"Where's he going?" Daniel said.

"To find Charlie. If he's right, he'll be with his brother."

"Okay, I'm really confused. I thought *Pinky* was a bad guy and *Charlie* wanted to *save* his brother."

"Don't think. Just help me get the deputy to safety. Somehow, we've got to stall this until Sheriff Stan gets here."

"How do you know he's coming?"

"Well, let's just hope he does, and soon. Now, let's get Mr. Pete moved before one of those Klansmen find him."

As they approached the logger man's tent, Charlie came out of the shadows.

"Where's the deputy, Hank?"

"What are you talking about, Charlie?" Hank said.

Daniel stepped back at the sight of a drawn pistol.

"Be careful, Hank, he's got a gun."

"Come on, Charlie, you can't be serious about being part of this."

"I thought he was one of the good guys," Daniel said to no one in particular.

Hank recognized the hurt in his best friend's comment. Then he heard a soft sigh coming from Charlie as the gun's barrel dropped slightly. His strategy shifted to concern. He wanted to reach out to the boy.

"What happened between yesterday and today to change your mind about these men?"

"Sometimes life doesn't give us the best choices. It's not as simple as you want to make it. Where's the deputy?"

"You're crazy if you think we're going to take you to him," Hank said.

Charlie clasped the pistol with both hands, leveling it at Hank and trying to keep it from shaking too badly.

"You don't understand, Hank. I *need* to find the deputy."

"What's to understand? I can't let you just waltz into that mob with Deputy Collins. I *won't* be responsible for putting him in more danger."

"What if a friend's life were at stake?"

"What are you saying? Are you being forced to do this?"

Fear flashed in Charlie's eyes.

"What if it were Daniel? Would you give up the deputy for him?"

"Ha!" Daniel said, his anger surprising Hank. "You think you're so smart, but you don't know anything. Hank and I aren't even friends anymore. Didn't you hear us arguing earlier? He could care less about me. Threatening him with me won't get you anything."

From out of nowhere a huge, dark figure stood behind Charlie. Daniel fainted. Hank stood still with his mouth open. Before anyone could speak, the giant wrapped Charlie in a hug that trapped the boy's arms close to his body. He wriggled like a fish out of water, trying to break free from the grasp. The pistol fell from his hands as his feet dangled at least a foot off the ground. As quickly and quietly as the giant appeared, it ran off with Charlie toward the river. It took several seconds for Hank to move. He collapsed to his knees when they would no longer support him. Daniel moaned then raised himself up on an elbow. He rubbed his forehead and shook his head as if he had just taken a swim in the river.

"What was that?" Daniel said.

"I don't know, but I think I've seen it before. Just not up close like that."

"Where's Charlie?"

"Whatever it was took him. I never heard it come or leave. Did you see the size of that thing?" Hank said.

"Did you see its face?"

"I think it could have been a man, but I'm not sure. It must have been nine feet tall."

"If not ten. Do you think it will hurt Charlie?"

"I don't know, but I'm not hanging around here, in case it comes back."

"You don't have to tell me twice. Let's get out of here. Do you remember where the deputy is?"

"Yeah, over here."

* * * * * * *

"Where is he, Daniel?" Hank began to hyperventilate.

"Are you sure it was this tent?"

"Yeah, at least, I think it was." Hank twirled in a complete circle, frantically trying to think. "They all look alike in the dark. It's hard to see the difference in them."

The boys searched each of the tents nearest the river, again, unsuccessfully.

"Maybe Doc hid the deputy after the cross was lit," Daniel said.

Another explosion of yellow fire lit the compound. Hank could feel the heat from the burning cross where they stood. "Let's go see what's happening."

They raced through the maze of tents to the front where all the noise was centered. When they reached the commotion, Hank wasn't prepared for what he saw. One of the riders had roped the big logger man and was dragging him behind a running horse. Colored women and children were crying in a large group near the first burning cross.

"No wonder these people are so scared. Look at the hoods they're wearing," Daniel said. "And I thought Granny Rose was scary."

"The horses are disguised, too, in case anyone recognizes them, I guess. They look as scared as these people are. How can anyone be so stupid to believe this is right? We need to do something, but what? If the *men* here can't stop them, what chance do *we* have against them?"

When the horse dragging the logger man returned, the man wasn't moving. There was a commotion from another large group of people near the second burning cross.

"Daniel, look. It's Dr. Warden."

He was breaking away from Pinky's friends to get to the man lying on the ground.

"If Dr. Warden's over there, where's the deputy?" Daniel said.

They didn't have to wait long to find out. Two other men without hoods dragged the still unconscious deputy between them.

"What are they going to do to him, Daniel?"

Panic filled Hank's heart with dread and fear. His feet felt like lead. They wouldn't move from their places.

"Where's the sheriff?" Daniel said.

"We can't wait. We've got to help Mr. Pete."

"But don't we need a plan, first? If we go in without a plan, we'll be no more help than the deputy."

Hank's body shuddered with fear and adrenaline.

"What are you thinking?" Hank said.

"Follow my lead. Maybe we can stall them long enough for the sheriff to get here. Pretend I'm one of Charlie's recruits."

Daniel grabbed Hank's arm and dragged him toward the mob.

"Hey, I've got another one over here," he said.

All eyes turned toward them. Hank searched the crowds for Pinky.

"I'll take care of him," one of the hooded riders said, galloping away from the group. He dismounted and stormed toward the boys. Hank's heart raced as the Klansman got closer.

"So much for hiding the deputy."

When Hank heard the voice, he jerked away from Daniel and snatched off the hood.

"Pinky," Hank said.

CHAPTER 16

Pinky gasped and quickly yanked his hood out of Hank's grasp, looking over his shoulders.

"Are you trying to get me killed?"

"I trusted you. I even defended you. Now, here you are one of them."

"No, Hank." Pinky's attention darted from Hank to the Klan and back, his eyes shining with unshed tears brimming close to overflowing. "I'm not. It was the only way to look for Charlie without their getting suspicious."

"Uh, guys? Look!" Daniel pointed a shaky finger in the direction of the doctor and unconscious colored man.

They all stared as several horses reared, a couple unseating their riders when a large man-like creature picked up the unconscious man and the doctor, throwing them each over one of its shoulders. It carried both men away quickly and quietly, just as it had Charlie just a short while ago. They watched it head toward the river.

"What in the world was that?" Pinky's breathing became heavy.

"Where's Mr. Pete?" Hank said. The edge to his voice caused it to crack, disbelief and desperation preventing him from maintaining his own control. "Where's the deputy?" He grabbed Pinky's shirt and heard it rip from the grip of his fists. "Were those your friends who had him, Pinky?" Their faces were a fraction of an inch apart. Hank could smell the sourness of Pinky's sweat.

"Yeah, they were taking him to the river." Panic replaced the fear in the older boy's voice. "It's easier to hide him there in the dark than around the light of those burning crosses. He'll be all right, Hank, I promise." Hank reluctantly released his hold and stepped away from him, studying the other boy's face and actions closely.

"What do we do till Sheriff Stan gets here," Daniel said, fear dripping from every word.

As Hank thought about the question, he watched the disorder that had developed. It looked as if everything and everyone were frozen in their places, except for the Klansmen's panicked horses. All movement was in extremely slow motion. None of the boys attempted to move. It was as if a thick, invisible cloud of fear shrouded the entire community. The three boys watched as the hooded riders fought to regain control of their animals and the situation. From another part of the compound, away from the commotion, another hooded rider kicked his horse savagely, riding hard toward the boys. When he was within a few feet of them, he dismounted and ran toward Pinky. He reached up and pulled the hood out of his hands.

"I thought something wasn't quite right about you. Where's my brother, Pinky?"

"Leave him alone," Hank said. Adrenaline took over his good, rational sense. He grabbed at the white tunic draped over Floyd Hutch's clothes.

"Stay out of this, kid. I'll deal with you later," Floyd said, yanking free of Hank's feeble grasp.

Pinky's eyes were wide, and Hank saw his Adam's apple bob just before he turned to run. Floyd grabbed one of the boy's upper arms and dragged him back toward the Klansmen.

"What are they going to do to him?" Barely controlled panic made Daniel's voice crack. "What are *we* going to do, Hank?"

"I don't know. We can't stop them, Daniel." He couldn't keep his eyes off the confrontation between Pinky and the Klan. "What would you do, Daddy?"

The silence in Hank's head roared as every word echoed off the walls of his mind. He realized his request for guidance was in vain. A dark dread trapped his ability to think. Then he heard the voice clearly, as if it came from someone standing between him and Daniel.

Hank, I'm here, son. You aren't alone. I'm standing right here beside you. I haven't left you.

Hank turned around in a circle, searching for the source of the voice.

"Daddy?"

Sweat began to drench his head, neck, shoulders, and back. His eyes stung, and his arms and spine tingled with electrified nerves.

You're here for a reason. Your daddy taught you all he was supposed to teach you. Now it's your turn to live the lessons and search for your purpose.

"Granny?"

"Hank, what's wrong?" Daniel said. "Who are you talking to? There's no one here but you and me."

Daniel's touch shocked him back to reality. Swallowing was hard. Hank's heart felt as if it were climbing up his throat. He looked at his best friend as if seeing him for the first time. He saw the alarm and confusion in Daniel's eyes.

"Daniel? Why are you still here? I don't want to see you get hurt, too. Please, I couldn't take it, on top of the guilt I'm already feeling, if something happened to you." Hank's panic felt like burning coals in his chest. He continued to wildly search all around him for the source of the voices inside his head.

"I'm not leaving you alone, Hank."

"Daniel, *this* is exactly what my daddy was fighting against when he died in France—hatred and injustice against people who don't deserve this kind of treatment. But I'm not him. I don't know what to do to protect them or you. This is all wrong. We can't fight this?"

Hank, remember, son. As long as there is evil, there will be war of some kind on earth, whether it's halfway across the world or right here in our own backyards. What is accomplished when someone dies is the guarantee there will be someone to take his place.

Hank put his hands over his ears and squeezed his eyes shut against the voices. His heart pounded loudly in his ears, but not loudly enough.

"What's wrong, Hank?"

Hank felt Daniel's hands on his shoulders and opened his eyes to see his friend standing right in front of him. He slowly lowered his hands to his sides, defeated.

"I don't know what to do." Sadness overwhelmed Hank's soul. He trembled. "I'm scared, Daniel. We're just kids. These men aren't going to pay any attention to us."

Your daddy taught you how to treat people and how to respect life. You are a special young man, Hank. I admire your friendship with Abraham because you don't see his color. You don't see my *color. You see past the obvious and go straight to the heart of who we are on the inside. Your daddy taught you that. You are keeping those values and beliefs alive and active in your heart. What* he *can no longer hold, that truth, to fight against evil, you are picking up to keep his cause from disappearing. There is a reason for you to continue where he left off.*

Hank searched the sky, his fists tightly clenched at his sides. "My feet won't move. I'm not brave like Daddy was or like Mr. Pete is. How am I supposed to carry on this fight without either of them here to help?"

Just then, a sharp crack split the air ominously.

"Hank, look." Daniel pointed toward Pinky and the Klansmen. One of the hooded men had a long bullwhip. Pinky was being tied to a tree, his back bared to the waist.

Before he could stop himself, Hank's legs were in motion with minds of their own. He ran the distance between Daniel and the Klansmen as if he were being chased by a mad dog.

"No-o-o-o!" Hank said. His breathing was hard when he stopped just a few feet from the man with the whip, but he didn't feel out of breath.

"Keep out of this, boy."

I know that voice. He's the leader of the Little Rock men.

"I said, leave him alone." Hank didn't recognize his own voice. He seemed to be floating above the scene, looking down on it as an observer.

"Hank, what are you doing?" Pinky said. "Get out of here before they hurt you and Daniel, too."

"Maybe you'd like to join him?" The Klansman had turned toward Hank and approached him with long, determined strides. He didn't blink as the man got closer, stopping abruptly just a foot or so away from him.

"Such misguided bravery. What a waste."

"What have we done to you? What laws have we broken?"

"How dare you question our right to be here."

"How dare you make yourself judge, jury, and executioner."

"Go home, boy, where you belong. Didn't your daddy teach you to respect your elders? This is none of your business."

"My daddy taught me plenty." Hank paused briefly, staring deeply into the man's eyes, unwavering, though every nerve inside shook savagely. "He taught me to step up and lend a hand when people needed help. He taught me to stand up for what's right and for truth. He told me that's what being neighborly was all about. He taught me that a man doesn't hide from doing the right thing or the truth. He taught me that a man stands up for those who can't because of injustice. He died doing just that." He could feel strength replace his trembling nerves. Warm courage filled his heart and soul as he firmly stood face to face with the angry Klansman.

"If what you're doing is right, why hide your faces?" Hank said, raising his voice so those in the back of the crowd could hear. "If you're really on the side of the law, why did you have one of your men shoot Deputy Collins? What you're doing here is wrong. You aren't doing the work of any real lawman. You're just trying to scare these people from their homes. They have a right to be here just like anyone else." Hank looked around at the frightened women and children from Beech Hill.

The man sneered before speaking. "Brave talk from someone who's just a kid. It looks like you're the only one who feels the way you do, though."

"No, he's not." Hank felt Daniel's presence to his right. "I don't like what you're doing, either. All you're doing is bullying people to make yourself feel important. You're not even from around here, are you?"

"Why, you little…" the Klansman said, raising the bullwhip over his head.

"You leave those boys alone," a woman behind Hank said. He heard movement from all around the compound. The Klansman froze in his threatening position. Hank turned to look at what frightened the man enough to stop him momentarily. Several of the children had come forward and gathered around him and Daniel, each carried sticks or rocks in their hands. Hank smiled and turned back to face the hooded man again.

"Looks like I'm not so alone after all. What kind of man waits to strike against defenseless women and children till he's made sure their men are out of the way?"

"That's a good question," Sheriff Stan said from the back of the crowd.

Hank jerked around at the sound of the sheriff's voice. He saw twenty or so men with rifles surround the compound while the sheriff stood to Hank's left.

"Take off the hoods," Sheriff Stan said. "Take them off or have them removed by my men. I want to see who I'm arresting here tonight."

After what seemed like an eternity to Hank, several men slowly removed their hoods. Hank recognized a few from Farmville. The rest were from Snow Hill, he guessed. There were still six who refused to remove their hoods.

"Gentlemen, do your duty." The deputies removed the remaining hoods, revealing the four Little Rock men, an older man that Hank assumed was Charlie's father, and another man he didn't know.

"Where's Pinky, Hank?" Daniel said, poking his shoulder.

Hank looked at the tree where the Snow Hill bully had been tied. There was no trace of the boy. "Sheriff?"

"We'll find him, boys. He can't be far. All right, folks, let's break this up, now. It's over. You can go back to your tents and your lives." As the crowd dispersed, the sheriff spoke softly to the boys. "I need to get you boys home, too. Hank, where's Pete, son?"

"Pinky said he was taken to the river, sir. The doc and another injured man were taken there, too, I think. If it's all right with you, though, we'd like to stay with you to the end."

"As long as I get you home in one piece, I guess your ma won't mind. Go on and go to him, boy. Tell Pete I'll be along shortly, after I get this mess cleaned up here."

"Yes, sir. Come on, Daniel."

The boys ran toward the river, using the trail they had seen the giant take.

"What if that thing has them prisoner, Hank? What'll we do then?"

"Somehow, Daniel, I don't think we have anything to worry about. My gut is telling me that thing was keeping the ones he took safe, or making sure they weren't hurt worse than they already were, even Charlie."

125

"I hope you're right."

Just as the two best friends reached the river, they heard the distinctive pump of a shotgun being prepared to fire behind them. They stopped abruptly, then slowly raised their hands and faced one another briefly before turning back toward the trail. Hank's lungs burned. He was unable to recall when he'd taken his last breath. There along the trail was a tall, shadowy figure with a double barreled twelve-gauge leveled at them.

CHAPTER 17

"WHERE'S CHARLIE?"

"You must be Floyd," Hank said, his heartbeat hammering a quick, steady tempo.

"So you know my name. Doesn't matter. Where's my brother?"

"What makes you think we know?" Daniel said.

"He was looking for you two the last time I saw him. He said you'd know where to find the deputy. That lawman was going to mess things up for us tonight. He had to be gotten out of the way. Charlie was supposed to find out if I killed him."

Floyd began to cry. Hank and Daniel looked at each other again briefly.

"Look, why don't you put that shotgun down," Hank said, softening his tone, feeling sorry for Floyd. "If you shoot us, how are you going to find Charlie? Put the shotgun down, and we can work together to find your brother and the others."

Floyd wiped his tears on his shirtsleeves. "It's just fine where it is. Besides, I don't care about the others. I just want to find my brother."

"Believe it or not, we do, too," Hank said. "We care about him as much as you obviously do. I don't want to see him hurt. Let's…"

"No, you don't know anything about us. Wait, hurt? Charlie's hurt? Why would he be hurt?"

"Didn't you see that thing back there?" Daniel said. "It got Charlie, too."

"What thing? What kind of trick are you trying to pull?"

"He's right. There was this…thing. It was really big and looked like a man, but…" Hank said, keeping his voice steady and calm. "Weren't you there when it came into the compound and took the doctor and the big guy that Klansman dragged?"

"What are you talking about? I got tired of waiting for Charlie, so I was searching the tents for him when I heard the commotion. When I saw you guys, I thought Pinky was my brother till I got closer. Besides, he has a gun. Why didn't Charlie just shoot whatever that *thing* was?"

"He didn't get the chance. It picked him up from behind, and he dropped the gun. That was the last time we saw him," Hank said, turning toward a movement that caught the corner of his eye in the woods near the trail.

Before anyone could react, the large man-like figure ran from the trees to where the three stood. It grabbed the shotgun out of Floyd's hands and broke it across its upper leg. It was so fast; no one moved. All the three could do was stare, open-mouthed as the incredibly tall creature tossed both pieces of the shotgun into the middle of the river. It then grabbed Floyd and flung him over its shoulder before running past Hank and Daniel. All either of them could do was watch it disappear along the trail they were using before Floyd stopped them.

"Did you see that, Daniel?"

Daniel just nodded his head, wide-eyed.

"It was a man. I'd bet you a hundred dollars it was," Hank said.

"You don't have a hundred dollars."

"How tall do you think he is?"

"How tall was Goliath?"

"What are we standing here for? Let's see where he goes with Floyd. Maybe the others are there, too."

Hank's legs hurt from running for so long without a break, but he didn't want to stop. When he realized Daniel wasn't beside him any longer, he stopped and turned to see his friend on his knees near the water's edge. His own heavy breathing was so noisy to his ears he could barely hear anything else. He walked back to his friend and collapsed beside Daniel in the sand.

"I'm sorry…Hank….I need…to stop…for a minute."

"That's okay….He's too fast….Do you know…where we are?"

They looked around, but nothing looked familiar to Hank.

"Have we been running in circles?" Daniel said, almost whining.

"No, but I can't figure out where we are in the dark."

As their breathing returned to normal, they went to the river and scooped the lukewarm water into their hands. Hank's tongue was so dry that he swished water around his mouth for several seconds before swallowing. He did that a couple of times, then he shook the excess water from his hands. They stood and looked around. The night noises came from every direction. Every now and then, a fish jumped in the river. Bullfrogs, crickets, and cicadas almost drowned out the distant call of a whip-o-will.

"What's that?" Daniel said, pointing toward a dim light just a little farther down river.

"Looks like it could be a campfire. Let's go, but not too fast. Try not to make too much noise."

The boys walked cautiously toward the light. As they neared its source, they heard voices.

"That's doc's voice, I think." Hank was guardedly relieved.

"Well, let's hurry, then."

Hank put a strong hand on his friend's chest.

"Wait. We don't need to go barging in without knowing what we're going into. I'll go around to the other side; you go in from this side. Be careful, just in case there's a problem. At least one of us needs to be able to go back for the sheriff if there's trouble."

"Okay. How will I know you're ready?"

Hank thought for a few seconds. "I'll hoot like an owl when I'm on the other side. You'll know it's me because it won't come from the trees. You go in first. If it's safe, I'll go in, too. If not, I'll run for the sheriff."

"Why can't I go for the sheriff?"

"Look, Daniel, I got us into this mess. I need to get us out of it. I won't leave you in danger. I need to do this, okay?"

"Okay, Hank. You be careful, too."

As Hank circled around the campfire, he heard more talking. There was a deep voice he didn't recognize, but the other was definitely Dr. Warden's voice. He didn't sound as if he was in trouble, but Hank didn't want to take any chances. He needed to find those he had put in danger and get them all back home safely. It took him several minutes to get in place before he hooted like an owl. He watched across the campsite as Daniel carefully revealed himself. Daniel's eyes got really wide when the giant stood. Hank saw the doctor smile and heard him introduce the big man to Daniel. The giant held out a massive hand for him to shake, but Daniel just stared at it. The giant grinned and ruffled Daniel's hair before leaving the light of the campfire. Doc showed a wide-eyed Daniel to a tent twice the size of those at Beech Hill. Hank's foot nervously shook while he waited for several minutes for Daniel to reappear from the tent. He waited for his friend go to the campfire and search for his hiding place.

"Hank, it's safe. You've got to come and see."

It must be okay. He's smiling. Hank slowly emerged from the foliage of the forest to the campsite. His heart beat so fast he thought it would burst from his chest.

"Is everybody here?"

"Yeah," Daniel said, smiling widely. "They're all here and they're all right—Charlie, Floyd, Pinky and his friends, Abraham and his mom, the man who was dragged behind the horse, and Deputy Collins. Doc said they're waiting for Sheriff Stan to get here before they move anyone. Charlie and Floyd are too afraid of the giant to run. It, I mean, he's gone to get the sheriff and show him how to get here. I think Sheriff Stan knows him from somewhere. I'm guessing prison. Oh, I almost forgot the best part. Guess what? It turns out we're not far from Granny Rose's."

Suddenly, Hank's legs felt weak and he became light-headed.

"Whoa, Hank, you don't look so good. Do you want me to get Doc Warden?"

He sat hard on the ground and cradled his head in his hands, resting his elbows on his raised knees. The heaviness in his heart and the weight on his shoulders were gone. He felt lighter than he had in weeks.

"I'll be all right. Just give me a minute."

I'm proud of you, son. You're strong, Hank—stronger than most boys your age. You have a powerful character that is being refined as you grow. Everyone around you is your teacher. People are put in your life for a reason. Don't try to find something that may not be there in everything you do, but make every experience count. Granny is right. Let her teach you wisdom. Deputy Collins is right. Let him teach you how to be the man you are meant to be. One more thing. Just because I'm silent doesn't mean I'm not near. Let the silence teach you how to slow down enough to think clearly and be patient.

"Hank?"

He jerked his head up at the doctor's concerned voice, as if rudely awakened from a deep sleep. *Did I fall asleep?* It took him a few seconds to remember where he was. Doc Warden was kneeling right in front of him, his large warm hand rested heavily on Hank's shoulder.

"Are you okay, son?"

He slowly nodded, unsure whether what he just experienced was real or not. He looked around for Daniel. No one else was around.

"Where's Mr. Pete? Is he going to be all right?"

"He's in the tent yonder. He's resting comfortably, thanks to our big friend's hospitality."

"Can I see him?"

"Sure. Go on in. He's still sleeping."

Hank got up, dusted off his backside, and took a deep breath before going to the tent. His hand shook slightly as he pulled the flap aside to enter. There was so much room inside with only a few pieces of furniture. The top of the tent was at least twelve feet high, he guessed. When he stepped inside, he noticed a couple of lit lanterns that kept the light dim but useful. It reminded Hank of the descriptions in books and stories of the hospital tents during the Civil War. Instead of a table, the deputy now lay in a bunk along the left side of the tent. Doc walked past him to the big muscular logger man in a bunk just beyond the deputy's. On the right side of the tent was another bunk where Abraham slept. His ma looked up and smiled as Hank came closer.

"Hi, Hank," she said. Her face was soft, and her eyes reflected peace.

"Hi, ma'am. How is he?"

"He's going to be just fine, thanks to you and those kind folks you brought with you."

Hank nodded. "When he wakes up, tell him Daniel and I will take care of things for Granny while he's mending."

He pulled up an empty chair beside the deputy's bunk and sat. Deputy Collins was lying on his side, with the injured shoulder up. Hank couldn't get rid of the thoughts that were in his head when Doc came to him outside just now. *Was that all a dream, or was it real?* Daniel pulled up a chair beside Hank and sat quietly with him.

"I thought you were gone," Hank said, shaking the cobwebs out of his head.

"Not without you. I told you I wasn't leaving without you, and I meant it."

"Daniel…"

"Don't, Hank. You weren't yourself. You were just protecting me…from what, I don't know. I don't need to know, and I don't want to know." He paused to take a deep breath and yawned.

"Tired?"

"Yeah," Daniel said, yawning, again. "You know, you aren't as dangerous as you like to think you are."

Hank smiled. "You're one in a million, you know that?"

"Yeah, that's what my dad tells me all the time. I keep wondering what he means by it, though." Daniel yawned again. "He's going to make it, Hank. Doc said he got shot in the best place possible because there's nothing to mess up that's important."

"Thanks, Daniel. That makes me feel better, but just a little. I wish he hadn't been hurt at all…none of you."

"You know, Hank, he's kind of sweet on your mom. Have you ever thought he might just be your new dad someday?"

"Would that be so bad?"

"I don't know. It could complicate matters if you think about it…when we're on a case, I mean."

"After the mess I made of this one, I don't know if I want to take on any more cases."

"Oh, sure, you will. I'll bet you it won't take you a month to find another one for us to investigate."

"You think so?"

"Yep. As a matter of fact, I already know of one you won't be able to let go."

"Really? What?"

"It'll wait. But if I were you, I'd make sure Beth Ann doesn't get left out of the end of the next one." Daniel rotated his left shoulder, and rubbed the muscle. "That girl can hit, let me tell you."

Hank chuckled.

"It would have been nice to have her here tonight," Daniel said. "You were about as scary back there as I ever want to see you. Where'd all that come from when you went nose to nose with that Klansman? One minute you were rooted where you stood, all scared and panicky and talking like a lunatic. The next minute you were sticking your neck out for Pinky. Of all people, Hank, why Pinky? Did you really have to help *him*?"

"I don't know. It was…" Hank shook his head, moving his mouth without forming words.

"What? It was what?"

"It was like I couldn't help myself." Hank thought a moment. "Do you think that's why my daddy helped that family in France? Maybe he couldn't help himself." They sat quietly for a few seconds. "I have a question for you."

"Shoot. Well, not literally, you know, it's just an expression…"

"Why'd you stand by me after how I treated you?" Tears threatened to overflow Hank's eyes while he watched his friend smile and shrug his shoulders.

"I couldn't help *myself*. You were a *little* outnumbered. I couldn't stay back and let you have all the fun."

"I'm really sorry for all those things I said. You're the best friend in the world to me."

"I know."

"Would you two *please* stop making so much noise and let me sleep?"

Hank and Daniel jerked their heads in the direction of Deputy Collins at the same time, wide-eyed and open-mouthed. Hank's heart skipped a beat or two till he saw the deputy open his eyes and smile.

"Mr. Pete, you're awake." Relief overwhelmed him emotionally. Tears flowed unchecked. "Do you need anything? Can I get you anything?"

CHAPTER 18

"I'M FINE. IT HURTS, BUT I'm alive. That's all that matters." The deputy's smile faded momentarily as he grimaced slightly.

"Yeah, but what's Ma going to say when she finds out I got you shot?"

"Hank…son, you can't blame yourself for my getting shot. I'm in law enforcement. It's bound to happen. Don't worry about your ma. I'll take care of her. She'll be okay. In a couple of weeks, this'll all be just a memory. How's Abraham?"

"He's over there. He's going to be fine, too." Hank sniffed and wiped his eyes. "Daniel and I are going to be around Granny Rose's for a while helping out till he's back on his feet. Who knows, maybe she'll hire us to help out after he's back to full health."

"Hank, don't even joke about that," Daniel said, his voice a bit edgy.

"Oh, Daniel, if you know how to keep her happy, Granny's as sweet as honey," Deputy Collins said.

"Yeah, well, we know where honey comes from, don't we?" Daniel said, his eyes getting round as he nodded his head slowly.

The deputy laughed then groaned and grimaced again.

"Careful, now." Hank gently patted the lower arm of the deputy's injured shoulder. "I'm glad you're okay, Mr. Pete. Come on, Daniel. Let's let him rest."

"We'll talk later, Hank." The deputy's serious look reminded Hank of one of his ma's. He nodded and stood to leave. His heart gushed with a spring of joy that gave Hank more encouragement than he'd experienced in quite a while. He smiled broadly while leaving the tent. *I'm actually happy about being in trouble. Maybe Daniel's right, and I* am *a lunatic.*

* * * * * * *

Pinky and his two friends were seated around the campfire talking and laughing when Hank and Daniel left Deputy Collins after nearly an hour. They stayed in the shadows and watched the three for several minutes.

"I'm still surprised and a little confused at your defense of Pinky tonight. What about the threats he made against you and your family?"

"Yeah, well, no one deserves to be mistreated, no matter who they are. And yeah, the threats were real. I just realized there were worse ones to deal with first when he told me what was really going on. If you think about it, bullies threaten because they're scared and don't know how to face their fears. Maybe it's better to help them by showing them kindness than by giving them the fight they're looking for. People *do* change, even Pinky."

"Are you going to call him on the stuff he threatened you with? I mean, how do you know he's not dangerous anymore?"

"Look at him and his friends, Daniel. They're no different from you and me. They just need someone to come along beside them and show them what caring friends are all about in the right way. Come on. Let's see if you can rub off on them." Hank stepped forward alone. He turned and waited for Daniel.

"You're serious? They still scare me…a little."

"All the more reason to be their friends, Daniel." They sat on driftwood from the river, across from Pinky and his buddies. All talking and laughing stopped immediately. After several minutes of silence, Hank rubbed the sweat from his palms on his trousers leg.

"Pinky, you've never told us your friends' names. You know me, guys. I'm Hank; and this, here, is Daniel." He stood to shake their hands.

"What are you doing, Hank Baker?" Pinky said. Neither of his friends would look Hank nor Daniel in the eyes.

"I'm just trying to offer you a friendly hand. We didn't exactly begin this friendship on level ground. You had a job to do. You were being forced to do the kind of stuff that keeps people from getting to know each another better. I want to give you guys the chance to get to know me and Daniel better, give you the chance to see us for who we really are. You asked me to trust you, in so many words, when things got tough back there. I'm asking you to trust me, now, to be a good friend who wants to get to know you better."

"What about all I said to you about your dad and your mom and the deputy? What makes you think I didn't mean it?"

"I don't, but I'm willing to think otherwise. I didn't give you much of a chance before, either. I admit I let my first impression of you keep me from being friendlier than I could've been. My daddy used to say that a stranger was just a friend we haven't met yet. I'm sorry I let my bad actions a few days ago get in the way of our being friends. I'm sorry you had to get into trouble to find out who really cares about you. I hope you know you can count on me to be your friend if you're in trouble, just like these two guys."

No one said anything for several minutes. The shorter of Pinky's two friends stood and offered to shake hands with Hank, then Daniel.

"I'm Arthur. My friends call me Arty. This, here, is Thomas."

"Glad to know you, Arty. Thomas," Hank said, shaking hands with both boys. "When he gets up and around, I'd like you to meet Abraham. He's a good friend of ours."

"And Beth Ann," Daniel said, shaking their hands, too.

"Oh, yeah, I'll introduce you to Beth Ann, too. Daniel and Beth Ann are about the best friends in the whole world."

"Why are you doing this?" Pinky said, wrinkling his brows, his eyes suspicious. "And while we're at it, why'd you stop them from whipping me?"

"Didn't you hear anything I said out there, Pinky? Doing the right thing isn't about the person. It's about doing the right thing because it's the right thing to do."

"I just don't understand you, Hank?"

"That's okay, Pinky," Daniel said. "Sometimes, I don't understand him, either. You get used to it."

After a few seconds of silence, all the boys laughed.

"I'm glad you weren't hurt, Pinky. Really, I am," Hank said. "The next time we come to Snow Hill, you need to show us around. How about it?"

Pinky looked at Daniel, nodded his head, and chuckled.

* * * * * * *

It was some time later when the boys heard several people coming down the trail toward the campsite. Hank's heart skipped a few beats before Sheriff Stan and a couple of his deputies walked into view. He let out the breath he'd been holding slowly then took a deep breath, surprised that his nerves were still on edge.

"I guess everything's back to normal at Beech Hill," Daniel said.

"No, it won't ever be *back* to normal," Hank said. "They'll just set a new normal till the next bit of trouble forces another new beginning."

Pinky, Arty, and Thomas stood when the men gathered around the campfire.

"Hey, boys. Is everything all right around here? Pinky, did they hurt you, son?"

"No sir." The boys shook hands with the sheriff.

"You all did a fine job. Thank you for helping us get to the bottom of this whole mess. I'm recommending that Clyde… Mayor Byrd give you each a reward for your part in capturing those troublemakers. Let me know if you *ever* need help of *any* kind. Don't get into trouble before you come and see me about a problem."

"What's going to happen to Charlie and Floyd, Sheriff?" Hank said, stirring the embers with a stick that smoldered.

"Well, their father's been arrested, and Floyd *will* be arrested for shooting Pete. For the time being, Charlie is a free young man. He was lucky this time. He was prevented from doing any real harm. Hopefully, his ma will be able to turn him around."

"Can Daniel and I see him before you take him away? Charlie, I mean?" Hank said.

"Sure. By the way, how's Pete?"

Hank waited till the sheriff sat beside him on the log. "He's going to be okay. He woke up earlier. Doc says he'll be all better in a couple of weeks."

"Good. Good."

"Sheriff, I'm real sorry I didn't tell you what was going on. I was afraid to get you involved. I was afraid you'd get hurt. I guess it was stupid to think you couldn't help. By not telling you, Mr. Pete got hurt, and could have been killed."

"You know, Hank, we all make mistakes. You did wrong by not coming to me with the threats. I could have saved you a whole lot of trouble. What I want you to do, and promise me you'll do it, is stop saying you're sorry and *show* me you've learned from all of this."

"How? My gut gets so sour when I think about all the trouble I've caused you and Mr. Pete and Granny. I'm afraid to go to sleep sometimes."

"Son, you're going to mess up. That's how you learn. Do you honestly think I don't have things in my life I wish I could change?

We all do. Learn to forgive yourself of the things that cause you so much grief. When it comes up in your mind after that, just let it go. It only has the power to cause you pain if you let it. I heard what you said to that twisted man out there tonight. I wish more *men* had the guts to speak their minds like you did. At least, I'd know where they stood. I wouldn't have to guess. You do your mom and dad proud, boy. You're a fine example for your little brother with your dad gone."

Hank's heart ached at the mention of his father. The pain and the guilt of the hurtful words he had said at his grave the other night cut deep. The anger at him for dying was lost to the acceptance that his life was finished, but his mission would live on in Hank. *I'm ready to let you go, Daddy. Rest in peace.* Unshed tears fell unchecked as Hank stretched his legs out in front of the campfire.

"You okay, Hank?" Daniel said.

"Yeah, I'm okay, better than I've been in a while. Give me a minute, and we'll go see Charlie before the sheriff takes him home."

* * * * * * *

"Okay, boys, I'll give you a few minutes with Charlie, then we have to go," the sheriff said, following the deputy escorting the manacled Floyd to a waiting motor car.

"You going to be all right?" Daniel said. "At least you won't have to worry about what your dad and brother are doing for a while."

"Yeah, I guess so," Charlie said. "You've got to believe me that I didn't want it to end like this. I wanted them to be different."

"Talk's cheap, Charlie," Hank said. "Is that what you really feel, or are you just saying that for our sakes?"

"What are you saying? Charlie's one of the good guys, isn't he?"

"I don't know, Daniel. Don't you remember the gun he held to your head? Which is the real Charlie? The one at Palmer's Grocery or the one out there tonight?"

"You know, Hank, not everything is as black or white as you want them to be." Charlie's chin quivered. Hank saw his pain and something he couldn't as easily identify reflected in the boy's eyes. "I love my dad and brother just like you do yours. But not everyone has a family like yours, squeaky clean and neat as a pin."

"Can you answer Daniel's question? Are you one of the good guys?"

"Define 'one of the good guys.' I've got to go." Charlie walked briskly away from the campsite, toward the trail the sheriff took with his brother a few minutes earlier.

"Wait," Daniel said, raising his voice. "We're your friends, Charlie. Whenever you need us, we'll be here for you. You can count on us."

Charlie stopped in his tracks, looking back over his shoulder without making eye contact. "Grow up, Daniel. Hank's right. Talk's cheap."

They watched the boy race out of sight, alone in the night.

"What did he mean by that, Hank?"

"Don't let it bother you, Daniel. You're the most honest person I know. You're loyal and sincere, and the best friend a guy could have. He'll see that and come around eventually. We have to believe that for him because he doesn't believe it himself right now. Let's get back to the tent. Morning will come soon enough, and Granny will be expecting us to get her chores done like usual."

* * * * * * *

Daniel was asleep on a cot toward the back of the tent where the injured logger man, Abraham, and Deputy Collins were resting till sunup. Hank sat beside the deputy's bunk. He couldn't sleep, no matter how hard he tried. He thought about all that had happened in the course of the past twenty-four hours. Thanks to Pinky, Sheriff Stan had already been aware of the trouble that was planned at Granny Rose's. Except for the excitement when Charlie arrived and the extra men on her property for the sake of appearance, the sheriff assured Hank and the deputy that all was well there.

Doc said the logger man's cuts and scratches would heal quickly. His ribs would be sore for a while, but nothing appeared to be broken. Hank was glad. He didn't know the man's name, but there was something about him that he had admired from the first time he saw him in Snow Hill. Abraham had awakened earlier and laughed, in spite of the pain, at Daniel's re-enactment of the events that took place at Beech Hill. Hank chuckled to himself as he thought about how Daniel could bring laughter into just about any situation.

"What's so funny?" the deputy said. Hank wasn't sure how long he had been awake, watching him.

"Just thinking about Daniel."

"He's a good friend. It's good to see you smile and hear you laugh, Hank."

"I guess it has been a while, hasn't it?"

"Now isn't the time, but we have some unfinished business between us."

"Yeah, I know."

"I'm not going anywhere, Hank. I want you to know you can trust me to be here for you and your mother and your brother. I'd like nothing better than to call you my son when the time is right, if you'll let me."

"I'll think about it."

"Hey, you two," Doc said. "Hank, you've been here at this bedside a lot since you got here. You need to get some sleep, son, and let this man rest."

"Okay. Good night, Mr. Pete."

"Good night...son." The deputy smiled. Hank nodded, grinned, and left, going outside once more before turning in.

Hank breathed in the predawn air and looked up. The clouds had cleared, and the sky was full of stars above the trees. He watched in wonder as a shooting star marked its fiery trail across the heavens. The night critters near the river were noisy. Yet, there was peacefulness in his heart that Hank accepted for the first time since his father's funeral last month. He turned to go back inside the tent when his eye caught a movement near the campfire. He saw the giant quickly and quietly enter the shadows of the trees. Before he was completely out of sight, he turned, smiled, and saluted Hank.

Who are you?